"Before my _____
anything bu _____

"Getting hurt chang __ you?

The look that came to his dark eyes told her that he realized she was interviewing him again, looking at angles, hoping for secrets.

"Do you ever take a break?"

"I've got five weeks left to turn in a manuscript that's as close to publishable as I can make it. I don't have time to—"

He stopped her with a kiss.

Her heart stumbled. Her breathing stuttered. Everything inside her woke up and glittered with happiness. She hadn't been here long enough to let herself imagine kissing him, but somehow she felt like she'd known him forever. For as attuned as he was to Max, she was as familiar, as accustomed, as understanding of him.

He pulled back. She blinked at him, his strong-featured face, his dark, sensual eyes. She should feel odd, uncomfortable or at least have the sense that kissing had been wrong. But nothing had ever felt as right.

"I've been wanting to do that all day."

Dear Reader,

Grant Laningham and Lola Evans's story hit me right in the heart. I know life's not easy. Trouble is part of the process and I expect my characters to take a few hits. Maybe even fail. But sometimes a hero and heroine come along who make you yearn to see them succeed. That was Grant Laningham and Lola Evans. In spite of their pain, each has mustered enough energy for a comeback.

But an unauthorized biography threatened to take Grant down, and a couple in France wanted to break up the new family Grant and Lola were forming with Max, the nine-year-old son Grant didn't know he had.

You'll root for Grant and Lola...and Max. Because really, all three need more than a second chance. They need a family.

Has the universe provided one? Or are they destined to have their hearts broken if the chips don't fall the way they should?

I think you'll love this story.

Susan Meier

Fling with the Reclusive Billionaire

Susan Meier

Recycling programs
for this product may
not exist in your area.

ISBN-13: 978-1-335-59650-5

Fling with the Reclusive Billionaire

Copyright © 2023 by Linda Susan Meier

For questions and comments about the quality of this book,
please contact us at CustomerService@Harlequin.com.

Harlequin Enterprises ULC
22 Adelaide St. West, 41st Floor
Toronto, Ontario M5H 4E3, Canada
www.Harlequin.com

Printed in U.S.A.

A onetime legal secretary and director of a charitable foundation, **Susan Meier** found her bliss when she became a full-time novelist for Harlequin. She's visited ski lodges and candy factories for "research" and works in her pajamas. But the real joy of her job is creating stories about women for women. With over eighty published novels, she's tackled issues like infertility, losing a child and becoming widowed and worked through them with her characters.

Books by Susan Meier

Harlequin Romance

Scandal at the Palace

His Majesty's Forbidden Fling
Off-Limits to the Rebel Prince
Claiming His Convenient Princess

A Billion-Dollar Family

Tuscan Summer with the Billionaire
The Billionaire's Island Reunion
The Single Dad's Italian Invitation

Reunited Under the Mistletoe
One-Night Baby to Christmas Proposal

Visit the Author Profile page
at Harlequin.com for more titles.

CHAPTER ONE

LOLA EVANS SAT on the bench seat at the back of a neat-as-a-pin sea cruiser while an employee of tech billionaire Grant Laningham steered the sleek boat. The mist from the wake would have ruined her thick dark hair, except she'd prepared for every kind of weather imaginable with her raincoat, umbrella, and hair in a ponytail. She hadn't needed the raincoat or umbrella, both were hooked over her arm. But her mom had always told her to prepare for every contingency, so she did.

The cruiser slowed. The captain expertly eased it to the dock and secured it. She rose and gave her head a shake, shifting her damp ponytail back and forth. With the heat of the South Carolina sun in June, even her thick hair would be dry in ten minutes.

Standing on the dock, the captain offered his hand to help her out of the boat. She took it with a smile. "Thank you."

Before she could add, "And thank you for coming to get me," Grant Laningham strode up the

gray boards of the weather-beaten dock, a yellow
Lab on his heels. Tall and lean, with piercing black
eyes and dark hair covered by a white Laningham
Lions baseball cap, he said simply, "Lola?"

"Yes." She extended her hand to shake his. The
power of his presence nearly overwhelmed her.
His face was perfect. Symmetrical angles and
planes and full lips. His oversize T-shirt couldn't
hide broad shoulders and thick biceps. His hips
were trim, his legs long.

He was tall, gorgeous and a genius.

With his yellow Lab sitting quietly at his side,
Grant shook her hand. "It's a pleasure to meet
you."

Though the urge to swoon or gush was strong,
she kept her composure. She wasn't here for fun.
She'd been hired to ghostwrite his autobiography.

Four years ago, Grant had been ousted from the
board of directors of the company he'd founded,
his wife had divorced him, and he had almost
died after being hit by a car. All in the space of
two weeks. He hadn't been interviewed by anyone since then. Actually, he hadn't been seen off
this island since he moved here to recover and do
physical therapy.

Now that he was ready to return to work, a
former employee had penned an unauthorized
biography that portrayed him as a narcissistic
workaholic who fired people at will, ruining careers. The tentative title was *Laningham the De-*

stroyer. The book was in the final stages, to be released in six months.

Giovanni Salvaggio, Grant's publicist, had decided the best way to combat it would be to release an *autobiography* first. The hope was people would want to hear Grant's story from Grant, and that even after the unauthorized biography came out, Grant's story would carry more weight.

But all that meant they had approximately six weeks to get a draft to his publisher.

No time for gushing or being a fan. They had to get to work.

"It's a pleasure to meet you, too."

Despite her best efforts to be objective, a swarm of butterflies took flight in her stomach. He was just so damned good-looking. Even better looking in person than in pictures.

But he was a perfectionist genius with a hot temper. Which was why his board ousted him. When his development team couldn't fix a glitch, he'd fired someone every day for a month. Every day every employee went to work not knowing if they'd have a job at the end of the day.

In an interview a week later, he'd unrepentantly told a reporter he'd done it to keep everyone on their toes—to motivate them. That had been the straw that broke the camel's back for his board, and he'd been fired himself.

Gorgeous or not, he was not someone a smart

woman got involved with. Especially not a woman who desperately needed this job.

She glanced around. Thick trees, some pine, some leafy deciduous, hid most of the private island. "Your home is amazing."

"Yes. It is. You can see why I chose to recover here after my accident."

She definitely could.

She brought her gaze back to his striking eyes. Once again, the power of his personality hit her like a sucker punch. That magnetic energy had bulldozed him through a lot of his life. She couldn't imagine him unable to walk, unable to work, virtually alone on an island he'd bought so no one would see him weak or suffering.

Grant motioned toward the path beyond the dock. "After you."

As she turned, the captain jumped on the boat and grabbed her luggage. Rather than give the bags to Lola, he carried them past her and Grant, heading toward a black wrought-iron fence. He didn't say goodbye. She didn't get a chance to thank him. Once he was through the gate, he disappeared into the thick foliage that arched over the stone path.

Grant didn't even acknowledge him.

But that was Grant Laningham: a brilliant man so focused that he barely noticed the people around him—

Which was why Giovanni feared the unauthorized biography. Despite how polite Grant was being with her, his business style and his behavior weren't for the faint of heart. Worse, since his accident, loss of control of his company and his contentious divorce, Grant had become even more difficult. Giovanni had warned her he would be sullen, moody and uncommunicative. But she was supposed to push past that. Get to the heart of who he was to make sense of his business style and clear his name. Should be a piece of cake to a woman who'd made her living as a journalist for nearly eight years before she bought a ranch and moved off the grid—just as Grant had.

Which was why she was more qualified to share his story than most people. As a recluse herself, she probably understood him in a way others couldn't.

The sound of an approaching boat filled the air. Lola glanced behind them to see another cruiser speeding toward Grant's dock. Apparently accustomed to water traffic, Grant seemed unfazed.

The noise got louder. Lola looked behind them again. This time Grant looked too. The cruiser slowed and pulled into the spot across from the boat Lola had ridden in on.

Cursing, Grant stormed back to the dock and strode to the cruiser.

She raced after him. She had absolutely no idea who was in that boat, but Grant Laningham didn't need any more enemies. Giovanni hadn't told her it was her job to keep him in line, but she was the one charged with writing a story that cleared his name. She didn't want to have to refute new allegations of bad behavior.

A short guy in a suit and round glasses hopped onto the dock, then he turned and helped a little blond boy of eight or ten up the few steps. The kid held a small stack of books, some of them chapter books, some of them coloring books.

Confused, Lola stopped.

Someone inside the boat slid two small suitcases and a backpack beside the little boy. The guy in the suit looked frazzled. The little boy never looked up.

"Who are you and what the hell are you doing here?"

The frazzled guy sighed heavily. "Grant Laningham?"

"Yes, I'm Grant Laningham! And you're on my island. *Private* property. Get back on your boat and be on your way."

"Is there somewhere we can talk?"

"No! How many ways do I have to say get off my island?"

In fairness this *was* a private island, but Grant was supposed to be fixing his reputation, not making it worse.

She stepped forward to try to smooth things over, but the man in the suit said, "All right. We'll talk here. I'm Oliver Fletcher. I'm an attorney in

New York City. I have in my possession the Last Will and Testament of Samantha Baxter. This young man is Max Baxter, Samantha's son." He paused to catch Grant's gaze. "Your son."

Lola's mouth fell open, as a look of absolute shock came to Grant's face. He didn't move. He didn't speak. It seemed like he couldn't.

She raced over to the small group. "You have Samantha's Last Will and Testament?"

"Yes." Fletcher passed it to Lola. "It explains why we're here." He pulled an envelope from his jacket pocket. "This explains everything else."

He handed the letter to Grant who took it slowly, his eyes never leaving the little boy.

Knowing Laningham the Destroyer would be denying this to high heaven if there wasn't a legitimate chance this child could be his son, Lola eased over to the little boy. "Max, right?"

He nodded, still looking at the ground.

Sympathy for Max swelled in her. He'd obviously lost his mother. If he was being brought to Grant by an attorney, Lola guessed that meant he was alone—as she had been when her parents died.

Her heart splintered. Especially when she realized he was being left with a stranger, someone Giovanni had warned her would be sullen and moody.

She slid her arm across Max's shoulders. "I guess you've been traveling a while."

The little boy nodded.

"Are you hungry?"

He pursed his lips and nodded again.

"We can take care of that." She turned Max toward the house. "I'm sure this house has a kitchen. Let's find it."

As she walked away, the lawyer continued speaking with Grant. "You have the will and the letter. I delivered Max, per Samantha's instructions. My responsibilities are now ended."

Grant ran his hand down his face. "Okay."

His easy acquiescence all but confirmed Lola's suspicions. He either had reason to believe this could be his child or he *knew* this was his child.

When he said nothing else, Lola stopped walking and turned to address the lawyer. "We're fine. We'll handle things from here. Thank you for bringing Max to us."

Fletcher smiled stiffly and got into his boat.

As the lawyer disappeared below deck, Grant Laningham rounded on her. "You do not speak for me!"

This was the real Grant Laningham. Not the extremely good-looking, polite guy who met her when she arrived. But the guy who fired people. The perfectionist who wanted everything his way.

She'd interviewed terrorists in Afghanistan. She was not afraid of a computer nerd. No matter how tall he was.

"I didn't speak for you. I gave Mr. Fletcher the

go-ahead to leave when you seemed too stunned to do it. Besides, you should be thanking me. I kept you from saying something you might regret. Especially right before you put out an autobiography trying to convince people you're a nice guy."

"I don't want to convince people I'm a nice guy!"

Oh, the narcissist was definitely back. "How else do you expect to combat the unauthorized biography?"

"With strongly wielded truth?"

She shook her head. "People will love to see you prove you are an angry, cantankerous man when you put out an angry, cantankerous autobiography. You'll just give credence to the other guy's book."

She eased Max toward the house again. "Grab his bags and I'll get him something to eat."

She heard Grant muttering but when she turned her head a fraction of an inch, she saw him pick up Max's suitcases and backpack. She and Max went to the kitchen and found a short, well-padded older woman.

"Well, good morning!" she said as Lola and Max entered.

"Hi, I'm Lola Evans. I'm going to be working with Mr. Laningham for the next few weeks," she said, introducing herself. "This is Max," she continued, giving the woman a look that told her not to question things. "He's here to stay with Mr. Laningham too. He's also hungry."

"I'm Caroline, Mr. Laningham's house manager. The cook has gone home for an hour or so before she has to start dinner, but I love to make breakfast for lunch." She smiled at Max. "Do you like pancakes?"

Max nodded eagerly.

As Lola set her raincoat and umbrella on an empty chair at a small table in the corner, Caroline guided Max to sit on one of the stools in front of the large center island of the huge kitchen. Restaurant-sized stainless-steel appliances sat among white shaker cabinets. A blue subway tile backsplash complemented the gray-veined marble countertops.

Heading to the stove, Caroline said, "What's your pleasure? Blueberry? Strawberry? Chocolate chip?"

"Chocolate chip."

Those were the first words Max had spoken and the sound of fear in his voice nearly did Lola in. It had been difficult enough as an adult to realize she was alone when her parents died. She couldn't imagine how terrifying it would be for a child.

Grant walked into the kitchen, addressing Caroline. "I left Max's suitcases at the bottom of the steps. I need to know which room to put him in."

Caroline glanced at Lola and said, "How about we put Max and Ms. Evans in rooms next to each other?"

Lola saw what she was doing. A scared kid in a strange house should be near someone kind and understanding. She might not be a part of Grant's personal drama, but she empathized with this little boy. For as long as she was here, she would try to make his transition easier.

"Okay. Sounds good."

The room grew quiet. Caroline retrieved a bowl and the ingredients for pancakes from the cupboards near the stove. "So, we landed on chocolate chip pancakes?"

Max nodded.

Grant looked at Lola. "Caroline is making him pancakes?"

"Yes."

"I haven't eaten lunch either Caroline. I'll have a few pancakes too."

"Absolutely." She caught Lola's gaze. "A pancake for you?"

"Sure." She'd hoped to have a minute or two alone with Max to help him acclimate, but she couldn't very well tell Grant to leave his own kitchen.

The room grew silent. Lola said, "I see you have books?"

Max nodded.

"What grade are you in?"

"Third."

"That's a fun grade. It was my favorite year of school. I had a really nice teacher."

Grant frowned at Max. "Shouldn't you be in school now?"

"It's June," Lola reminded him pleasantly. "Schools are out for the summer."

"Oh. So, you'll be in fourth grade in the fall?" Max nodded.

There were a million questions she wanted to ask. Had his mother been sick? Had she been killed suddenly? What had this poor child gone through over the past few weeks?

She didn't want to put him through anything else or say something that might upset him. But she needed to get answers so neither she nor Grant inadvertently hurt him.

She took out her phone and typed in Samantha Baxter, Manhattan. Hundreds of entries popped up. She clicked on the obituary and discovered that Samantha had died and been cremated only two days before. Apparently, she'd been in an accident. Which meant Max hadn't suffered watching his mother die, but he had lost her suddenly.

And only two days ago. He hadn't even had time to grieve.

"Here you go," Caroline said, setting a platter of pancakes on the counter.

Lola noticed that dishes had magically appeared while she was searching Max's mom. She took a plate and served him a pancake, then handed the syrup to him.

"Thanks."

"You're welcome, sweetie." Lola's eyes filled with tears.

This poor child. His mom was gone, and he was stuck with a guy who wanted to write a biography that made people dislike him even more than they already did.

This was not going to go well.

CHAPTER TWO

AFTER THEY ATE, Lola suggested she and Max swim. Caroline led them upstairs to their rooms so they could change into swimsuits. Grant headed to his office.

Pulling the explanation letter out of his back pocket, he sat on his big office chair. He leaned back and took the thin sheet of paper out of the envelope.

Dearest Grant,
I prepared this letter in the event that some-
thing should happen to me. If you're read-
ing it, I'm either hospitalized or gone. I hope
I'm not gone.

His eyes unexpectedly filled with tears. He could hear Samantha's voice as he read her words, remember her sense of humor and her zest for life. If he hadn't met his wife a few days after the business trip in New York when he and Samantha had worked together, he would have continued seeing her.

And his life would have been so much different. He and Samantha might have stayed together. He would have known Max from infancy. He wouldn't have married his ex. The decisions he'd made that got him kicked off his own board might not have been made. Hell, he might not have walked out in front of that car—

He took a breath. Speculation and second-guessing never helped anyone.

You'd already met your wife by the time I discovered I was pregnant. Both of our lives were complicated enough. I believed I had done the right thing by keeping Max to myself. I hope you understand.

He did. Sort of. Samantha had been extremely levelheaded. Not just smart but filled with common sense. If she'd chosen to raise Max on her own, it had been with thought and good intentions.

I have relatives in France, a cousin and her husband. Max and I have visited them for most holidays. He knows them.

The words stopped.
He flipped the page over. Nothing.
That was it? A mention of some relatives?
He couldn't tell if Samantha didn't know how

to end the letter or if this had been a draft she'd planned to finish later.

It made the most sense to assume she'd put this draft with her will, intending to complete it later. She'd probably thought she'd had all the time in the world, as he had the day that he'd nearly been killed by the car that hit him.

Obviously, she'd died suddenly, or she would have finished it.

Lola Evans would know.

Not only had Fletcher given the will to her, but also Grant had seen her on her phone while Caroline was making their pancakes. She'd probably searched Samantha's name.

Overwhelmed, he ran his fingers through his hair. He could not believe he was a father, but the timing was right. If Max was his child, he would be nine years old. That corresponded with the two weeks he'd spent with Samantha.

And he knew Samantha wouldn't lie.

He left his office and went out to the pool area. His yellow Lab, Benjamin Franklin, had joined Max in the pool. The dog loved to swim, and Max seemed to be totally smitten with the dog. If nothing else Ben was a good diversion while he talked to Lola.

He saw her sitting on a chaise, her eyes glued to the little boy and the dog. Her blue one-piece swimsuit accented every soft curve of her body, and he swore his mouth watered. With her bountiful black hair and beautiful face, she was stunning enough to make him stutter or trip over his own feet.

Which was incredibly bad timing. Not only was it inappropriate to be attracted to an employee—he'd learned that the hard way with his ex-wife—but the situation with Max had to take precedence.

He sat on the chaise beside Lola's. "What did you find out when you searched Samantha?"

"She died two days ago."

He groaned. "Two days ago?"

"After Max got in the pool, I dug a little deeper and found the report of an accident in the paper. She was walking past a construction site, and something fell."

"Oh. God." He took a long, slow breath as he absorbed that. "She was a really great person. But I met my wife a few days after I returned from the trip where I'd met Samantha. We'd spent two weeks together, but once I met my ex, I was… occupied."

She shook her head. "Unless you want this going into your autobiography don't paint a picture."

He snorted. "Yeah, well, the fun didn't last."

"So I've heard."

He grimaced. The whole damned world had heard. "Anyway, I read Samantha's letter. It's fairly straightforward. She doesn't go into detail or even make an argument about why Max is mine.

She simply explained that I'd met my wife by the time she realized she was pregnant, and both of our lives were too complicated for her to tell me."

"What you're saying is you believe her."

"Yes."

"You'd still be wise to have DNA verification."

He agreed, but the realization of being a father suddenly overwhelmed him again. "I had the worst parents in the world. I have no clue how to be a dad. My sister and I basically raised ourselves and if the rumors are true about me being a crappy human being, it looks like I didn't do such a great job."

"I don't know how to tell you this, but you don't have any options. You can't abandon this child."

"I know…but Samantha's letter mentioned that she had relatives in France, people Max knows. I think we should pay them a visit."

She gaped at him. "You also can't dump that little boy off on distant relatives in a strange country."

"They aren't distant relatives. They are cousins—Max knows them. Samantha said they had spent holidays with them. Max may actually prefer living with them. I'm the stranger here."

She sighed, as if seeing his point. "Maybe."

"Look. Samantha wasn't a gold digger or opportunist. She was a highly paid lawyer in Manhattan. She didn't say things lightly. The letter must have been a draft because it ends abruptly. And the paragraphs are sort of disjointed, as if she was trying to figure out what to say. I'm guessing it was in her estate planning file, and it had enough information that Fletcher brought it with the will."

"Okay."

He took a breath. "With the letter unfinished, the mention of distant relatives might mean something. She might have wanted to suggest I let them raise Max. She knew how busy I was. She knew my life was complicated…and public." Suddenly realizing Samantha's reasoning, he groaned. "*Ridiculously public.* When I'm out and about, I'm hounded by paparazzi. My best guess is that she didn't want her son raised by me at all but hadn't gotten around to putting those wishes on paper. Did you read the will?"

"It's all standard stuff. Liquidate her assets. Pay her expenses. Everything that's left goes into a trust for Max."

"She didn't say she wanted him to be raised by me?"

"No. But she also didn't say she wanted him to be raised by the cousins in France."

"That might have been part of how she intended to hide him from the publicity that surrounds me. Wills get filed. Private letters do not. If she named those cousins in the will, everybody would have known who they were—and would have known where Max was."

"That's true."

"There has to be a reason she put them in that letter."

"Maybe she just didn't want him to lose touch with his extended family?"

"Maybe." He sighed. "I can't help thinking she knew me well enough to realize I wouldn't be a good dad."

Convinced that was her motivation for telling him about the cousins in France, he pulled out his phone and called Giovanni, putting it on speaker so Lola could hear.

"Hey...what's up?"

"Lola and I are going to be taking a quick trip to France."

"Oh, no! No. No. No. Look Grant, I know she's pretty but—"

"It's not like that." His brain stalled. She was pretty enough, subtly sensual with her dark hair and nice curves, that he wished it *could* be like that. But she was an employee. His ex had bowled him over the same way. He knew better now than to act on those feelings.

"I have some unexpected personal business in France. We need to handle it."

Lola's sapphire blue eyes widened to the size of small cookies. She shook her head at him and mouthed, "I am not going with you," as Giovanni said, "You can't go to France."

"Look, Gio, I don't have a choice."

"Yeah, well, the publisher putting out the un-authorized biography got wind that you're writing your own version to contradict it, and they've upped their pub date. If you want to beat that book to stores, there is no wiggle room. There's no time for a draft. We're lucky Lola's a professional, meaning editing should be minimal."

Lola mouthed, "No draft?"

Grant said, "No draft?"

"No draft. Whatever you turn in gets edited, you and Lola get approval after that to make sure nothing got messed up in editing, then we go to print."

"What happens if I don't beat him, and we put out my book a few weeks after his?"

"Then your autobiography looks like a desperate attempt to answer everything in his book. It won't look authentic or like you're penning your story. It will stink of desperation."

"Damn it!"

Lola motioned to Max and shook her head.

Grant groaned. "I only said damn it. Not anything earth-shattering. I'm sure he's heard it before."

Giovanni said, "Who's heard what before?"

"The dog has heard the word damn before. He's in the pool but Lola thinks he heard me."

Lola's eyes widened again at the way he evaded the truth. But he wasn't ready for anyone to know about Max. Hell, he hadn't adjusted yet. He needed time as much as Max did.

Gio sighed. "Look, Grant. I don't know what you and Lola are doing, but you've gotta get that book out. Six weeks might be tight, but if you two actually worked you could get it done."

Grant stopped a genuine curse. With so much riding on this, he saw Giovanni's side, albeit reluctantly. "All right. Fine. I hear you."

"You're the one who wants to go back to work."

He did. For the past year, his brain had been coming up with ideas that couldn't wait. New technology could never wait. But having to mend his reputation had taken on an entirely new meaning. Even if he didn't have to raise Max, he had to protect him. He had the kind of life that the paparazzi lived for. They followed him, took pictures from boats only a few hundred feet off the beach, trying to get shots of him limping or struggling with a walker—which was why he had so many plants around the house, especially the pool. If they discovered he had a son, a son he hadn't known about, and that poor Max's mom had died, Max's life would be fodder for the press.

Giovonni's voice brought him back to the present. "You put your book out first. Don't make yourself a saint, but don't make yourself a jerk either. Be honest. No hiding things. Set the record straight on why you fired so many people that your board ousted you. Talk about your wife's affairs. Admit you were an arrogant workaholic and let's get this ball rolling!"

With that he hung up and Grant sat staring at the phone.

"He wants you to admit you were an arrogant workaholic?"

He peeked up at her. "My board ousted me. My wife had numerous affairs. I *was* a workaholic. Responsible for my board's decision and maybe my wife's infidelity."

"This is going to be some book."

Sure. Right. He would be dictating all his secrets to one of the prettiest women he'd ever met. Someone smart enough and kind enough to be good to Max—

That should not bother him. He'd made his decisions about his ghostwriter. She was off-limits.

So why did he feel like scowling? Lola might be beautiful and sweet, but she was an employee. Plus, he knew relationships were a disappointing trap. He should just ignore her.

And he really did need help with Max.

"You didn't want to hire me, did you?"

Her question surprised him into looking over at her. She wore the expression interviewers wore when they wanted to catch someone in a lie.

"Honestly, Lola—" The feeling of her name on his tongue sent the weirdest feeling skittering through him. He shook his head to clear it. "I told Giovanni I wanted a bulldog. I wanted someone to put enough punch in this thing that I didn't look like a wimp. I don't want to look like the jerk my former employee is trying to make me out to be. But I also don't want to look like I've got my tail between my legs. I'm edging myself into a business world that's moved on without me. I have to show people I'm still strong. I want this book to have some teeth."

Her chin lifted. "I can make it bite back."

"You better because it sounds like I don't have time to hire someone else."

He rose from the chaise and turned to leave.

"Where are you going?"

"Inside. To work."

"You can't leave Max out here by himself."

"You're here."

She shook her head. "Nope. Don't go there. Like I'm a woman so I automatically get kid duty. I'm happy to help you while I'm here. But my end of this book will require twice the time your part of it does. Plus, he is *your* son. Lesson one in parenting is that you are bottom-line responsible. And whether you like it or not he needs you."

"Okay. So, what does our schedule look like then? How are we going to write this thing?"

"After hours in a pool, kids sometimes take naps. They like to play on their own sometimes. Especially video games. Plus, it looks like he's making friends with your dog. We'll work when he's on his own. Then you play with him when he wants company and I'll start writing from whatever notes we make in the morning."

He raised his eyes to heaven.

She rose from the chaise. "You know, an interesting angle for your autobiography might be to write it around the fact that you got custody of a child you didn't know you had and how it changed you."

The very thought horrified him. "First, I won't be putting Max into the book. While I'm growing accustomed to being a dad, he's also getting accustomed to a really bad situation. I don't want to make that worse. Second, he might *choose* the Paris relatives over me and then if people know about him but don't know the whole story, I'll look like a guy who dumped his son on relatives. Third, not putting him into the book is the best way to protect him."

She laughed. "Look at you. You do have some parental instincts."

He gaped at her. "Was that a test?"

She ambled up to him and smiled. All his male hormones woke up. Along with a yearning for something he couldn't have. He told himself that was the truth of it. His interest piqued because she was an employee, off-limits the way his ex should have been. But he'd also been on this island for four long years. He'd had a few visits from friends and lovers and women his friends brought to spend time as a group, having fun.

But none of that felt like this. Fresh. Unique. Full of potential.

"No test. The biggest part of my job is to figure out the angle for this story. I'll be questioning the life out of you and running ideas past you for the next four weeks."

He took a breath to settle his hormones. "We have *six* weeks."

"And I'll need the last two to edit what we put together in the first four weeks. I told you. I'm going to be busy." She glanced around at the pretty day. "Sunny or not, it looks like I'd better set up the office area in my suite today."

She walked away and he scowled at her, then the scowl turned into a frown.

She was not going to let him walk all over her.

Maybe she was a bulldog after all?

The thought pleased him a little too much. His wayward brain pictured all kinds of ways she would be fun to have around, fun to tease and flirt with—

Benjamin Franklin hopped out of the pool and shook himself spraying Grant with cold water, as if he knew it was his job to bring Grant back to reality.

Max looked at him with big, frightened eyes.

"Hey, it's okay. People who stand by pools have to accept the fact that they might get wet."

Max nodded and Grant forgot all about his pretty ghostwriter. His chest filled with pain for the scared kid in his pool. How was he ever going to help this child?

CHAPTER THREE

LOLA SET UP her laptop in her suite on the third floor and pulled assorted files on Grant's life out of her suitcase. She could have stayed in her room another hour. Given that she'd traveled from Montana to South Carolina that day—having to rise at three o'clock to make her flights because of the difference in time zones—what she really needed was a nap. But she couldn't abandon Grant.

Or Max.

Max was the one who really needed her. Grant was the one who scared her.

Not because he was grumpy. Because he was interesting. Sexy. Smart. Overconfident. He would be tremendously fun to tease. But teasing a client was all wrong. Being attracted to him was even worse. She would control both because this job would stave off bankruptcy for a few months—maybe even a year. Her ranch wasn't supporting itself and she had to earn big chunks of cash to keep herself from losing everything she had.

Also, Max needed a levelheaded person to steer

Grant in the right direction. If she believed in fate or destiny, she would assume she'd been sent here to help Grant with Max. Not to flirt. And certainly not because of some starry-eyed wish that Grant was her Prince Charming. She didn't believe in a glitzy, fancy, famous Prince Charming. She wanted a nice, normal guy who would settle her life not fill it with controversy.

With her work area assembled, she returned to the pool. "If there's anything you need to do, I'll watch him."

Grant rose from his chaise lounge. "Actually, I do need to make some arrangements with Caroline."

He glanced at Max, looking like a guy who didn't want to leave, and her heart tugged. He might have had bad parents, but he definitely had good instincts.

"I also think we need to do the DNA sooner rather than later."

She agreed. "If there's a mistake of some kind, it's best to find out now."

He nodded, then went into the house.

She slipped out of her bathing suit cover-up and jumped into the pool. "What's the dog's name?" she called to Max.

He laughed. His short yellow hair had spiked from being wet. His blue eyes were filled with little-boy excitement.

Never underestimate the power of a dog with a child.

"Benjamin Franklin."

"I don't think your dad knows how to name a pet. Maybe we could think of a cool nickname?"

Max shrugged.

"No hurry. I'm sure a name will come to us. Let's play a game." She found a Frisbee and tossed it. Unfortunately, a breeze caught the red disc, and it landed on the sidewalk on the other side of the pool. Benjamin Franklin leaped out of the water to retrieve it and brought it back to Max.

The dog really seemed to like the child. Max liked the dog; the dog liked Max. This was the bridge they needed to help Max adjust.

She called, "Throw it again. We'll see what he does."

Max nodded and tossed it to the deep water near the diving board. Benjamin Franklin swam after it.

They spent the rest of the afternoon that way and Lola was glad. When Max came downstairs for dinner, he seemed tired enough that he probably wouldn't have trouble sleeping.

They ate mashed potatoes, chicken and broccoli, followed by cherry pie. By the time they were done, Max's eyes were drooping. They took him upstairs and found pajamas in one of his bags.

He quietly said, "My toothbrush is in the backpack."

Grant unzipped it. "Got it."

Pajamas and toothbrush in hand, Max went into the bathroom. Two minutes later, he came out in PJs decorated with characters from a popular video game.

Lola tucked him in. "You know, if there's anything you want to talk about, we're here for you."

He nodded. His eyes filled with pain that made her heart stumble.

Grant said, "Yes. We're here."

Still tucking the blankets around him, Lola softly said, "I'm very sorry about your mom."

Max blinked back tears but said nothing. Lola could only imagine his confusion. Two days ago, he had a mom and probably lived a totally different kind of life in Manhattan. Now he had a dad he didn't know, a swimming pool and a dog.

Grant walked around to the other side of the bed and sat beside Max. "I really liked your mom. She was a great person."

Surprised, Lola peeked at him.

"If there's anything you want to talk about, even if it's only to tell stories about her, I'm here. So is Lola." He paused a second. When Max didn't say anything, he added, "Lola and I are going to be working on a project together, but we'll both be spending time with you."

Max nodded. His voice shook just the slightest bit when he said, "Okay."

"Do you know anything about me?"

"My mom said you were smart, and I'll probably be good at math."

Lola bit back a laugh, but Grant chuckled. "Your mom was very smart too. Nine chances out of ten, you're going to be downright brilliant."

Max smiled.

Lola's eyes filled with tears. Not from compassion for Max, but because Laningham the Destroyer was trying to be good to Max in a simple way that ended up being profound.

Grant rose. "Okay. You get some sleep."

Lola said, "Good night."

Max said, "Good night."

They stepped out into the hall and Lola just stared at Grant. "You have parental instincts like nobody I've ever seen."

He led her to the steps. "I told you I raised myself."

And had really bad parents. In her research, she'd discovered they were both doctors, both retired now in the Florida Keys. Both had won commendations. Both had chaired hospital committees and been department heads. She could see where they wouldn't have had time for parenting. She could also see this was a huge part of Grant's story. She simply wasn't sure how yet. Especially if she wasn't permitted to mention Max in the book.

They started down the stairs. Grant said, "I'm going for a short walk on the beach."

Eager to ask him questions while he seemed to have his guard down, Lola said, "I'll come too."

"You think Max will be okay alone?"

"Maybe we shouldn't walk on the beach. Maybe we could just grab a couple of beers and sit by the pool. Tomorrow we'll get a monitor for his room, so we can make sure he's okay if we want a walk."

Grant took a breath. "You're going to interview me, aren't you?"

"Yeah, but in case you haven't figured it out, I've been observing you all day. My work started the minute I stepped onto your dock."

"Great. You witnessed the most unexpected event in my life—discovering I have a child. In one odd day, you know more about my personal life than most people ever will."

"Not after your autobiography is released."

He groaned.

She slid her arm under his and led him toward the pool area. "Let's go get that beer."

He desperately wanted to say something snarky, at the very least swear her to secrecy. But the way she slid her arm around his sent electricity sizzling through him, forcing him to raise his guard again. She was a reporter, trying to establish a rapport so he'd open up to her. Nothing more. He was the one with the attraction problem.

He walked her to the patio. Lights from the

pool dimly lit the area, making it a peaceful, private oasis.

"Have a seat. I'll get the beer. Do you have a preference?"

"Whatever you have is good."

He laughed. "I have everything. My college roommates like to pop in uninvited. I'm always prepared."

She named a brand of light beer. He pulled two bottles from the fridge in the outdoor kitchen.

Sitting on the chair beside hers at the round patio table, he handed one to her.

"Thanks." She nodded toward the darkness. He'd left one six-foot swatch of land clear of plants so they could see down the beach, but the ocean was absorbed into the black night. The sound of the waves was the only indicator there was water beyond the sand. "This is beautiful. So peaceful."

"Who says money doesn't buy happiness?"

She laughed. "Probably you, since I get the feeling you haven't been happy a lot."

He grunted. "Who is?"

"Good point." She took a drink of her beer. "Why don't we start at the beginning? Tell me about your parents."

It was the last thing he wanted to talk about. He couldn't think of his parents without thinking of his sister and he refused to go down that ugly road. That was one secret that would never see the light of day. He intended to keep his family out of his autobiography. Especially since he didn't see them as part of his story. His life had begun when he finally finished his degree, got his first job and left his parents' house for good. No reason to mention them.

"I thought you would have researched them."

"Of course, I did. But I want to hear the story from you."

"It's going to be short because there's not much to tell. My parents were successful physicians who constantly told my sister and me that *this* was what success looked like."

"This?"

"Their lifestyle. Work all day, then chair committees and fundraise all night."

"Leaving you and your sister alone?"

"No. We had babysitters. But one night when the babysitter was on the phone with her friends, I looked around and I thought *this* is boring. And *this life* doesn't feel like success. I'm not doing *this*."

"But you did do that. Actually, you surpassed your parents' accomplishments."

He grinned. "Yeah, but I'm not a doctor. That's what they wanted me to be. To follow in their footsteps. To keep the family legacy alive."

She laughed. "You might not be a doctor, but you *are* successful."

"In my way and on my own terms."

She thought for a moment, then she said, "What terms are those?"

"I work for myself, not a hospital or a charity. And I don't do what I do for applause or admiration. I work to change the world."

"And that makes you happy?"

"Not in the way you mean. Everybody gets bursts or moments of happiness, but I think the best a person can be is content and using my intelligence makes me content, fulfilled."

She said nothing, apparently thinking that through. Lights shimmering off the pool glistened around her. With her hair out of the ponytail, falling around her face to her shoulders, accenting her pretty blue eyes, she looked ethereal. Like a goddess.

Attraction rose again. Her interview style was more like a conversation than a reporter digging into his life. In the dim lights, with the world around them a silent place, he was comfortable—the very last thing he expected to be when talking about details that would form his autobiography.

Except he didn't feel like he was giving details. He felt like he was talking with a friend.

"What about you? What's your life like?" The question popped out before he could stop it, but now that it had, he was glad. He'd researched her enough to know she'd been on her way to the top at a network news outlet, then her parents had been murdered and she'd dropped off the face of the earth. Giovanni had had the devil's time finding her.

His curiosity about her knew no bounds, and when he got curious about something he couldn't stop his brain. Given that they were working together he could also make asking about her life sound legitimate. Not like attraction-driven curiosity—though most of it was. "If I have to trust you with intimate details of my life, I should at least know who you are."

"I'm sure you know the important things."

"Like your parents were murdered? Or that you left your job?"

"Either or. That's about the extent of the items of interest in my story. Both were reported on network news because back then I was a celebrity of sorts."

"I also read that you bought a ranch."

"That was long enough after I quit my job that it didn't make the network news." She took a swig of beer. "Meaning, you investigated me."

"I'm trusting you. I had to be sure I could."

"Then you know my ranch is on the brink of bankruptcy."

"It's a tough time for that business."

She looked at him skeptically. "You know about ranching?"

"I know about the stock market, price indexes and real estate. The rest is normal deductive reasoning."

She shook her head. "I suppose now you're going to tell me you know a little bit about everything?"

He laughed and sat back. "Pretty much." He drank some beer then said, "My mind has a thing for details. It loves them. It's how I can think down the board for an answer while everybody else is still stuck in the problem. The more intricate the subject, the more clues my brain can find to improve either a product, a strategy, or a system."

"Makes sense."

"What about you?"

She glanced up at him again. "What about me?"

"What are you good at?"

She held his gaze. "Reading people."

Challenge sizzled through him. But not in the way it did when he got an idea to best a business opponent. This was sharp, sexual, and definitely wrong. But so delicious he couldn't help indulging just a bit. Flirting. Egging her on.

He smiled. "I made a living out of keeping my thoughts to myself."

"With a bunch of amateurs maybe. I'm a pro. I've interviewed bigger, badder, scarier people than you. I'll see right through a lot of your crap."

He laughed. This could be so much fun if he actually had time to make her work for every tidbit that he had to tell her. But they didn't have time and he had a child to attend do.

Still, the urge to flirt wouldn't be denied. He held out his beer bottle to tap hers in a toast. "Here's to you trying to get my secrets. And failing."

Rather than scowl, she laughed. Really laughed. As if the sea breeze filled her with joy.

In less than twelve hours he more than liked her. She held her own with him. She made him think. She made him *laugh.* Even bogged down by the fact that he had to counteract the lies in an illicit telling of his life, compounded by discovering he was a father, she made him relax.

She was also oh, so pretty. Pretty enough that he wished they were walking on the beach, and he was sweet-talking her. Pretty enough and interesting enough that he knew a fling with her would be the most memorable of his life.

Except he needed her. Not only did he want her to write a strong autobiography, but also, she was good with Max. Sympathetic without being condescending. Max needed her.

Which was why he'd already decided she had to be off-limits.

Now he would have to figure out how to be as close with her, as intimate about his life as he'd have to be to pen an autobiography, without all that closeness tipping over into something more.

She finished her beer. "It's been a long day for me. I'm going to turn in."

"Okay." He rose from the table. "I'm heading

inside too. Maybe I can find a Laningham Lions baseball game on TV."

"You don't know when your own team plays?"

He shrugged. "Bought the team as an investment. Then I started liking baseball." He shrugged again. "But it's not an obsession."

He followed her as she walked to the door and into the ground-floor family room filled with thick couches, three televisions and a pool table.

Inside, she paused and turned to him. "Good night."

Standing six inches away from her, he let himself enjoy her smile, her pretty eyes. The moment froze in time. It would have been the most natural thing to kiss her good night. He wanted to. Every fiber of his being felt drawn to move in the few inches between them and press his lips to hers. He knew they'd be good together—

The reminder that the last time he'd felt like this had been with his ex-wife filled his brain. She'd burst into his life, the new receptionist at his company, and what had sparked between them was just like this. Happily sexual. They'd laughed as much as they'd made love. From the minute he'd seen her, he hadn't been able to keep himself from flirting. He'd had the unquestionable sense that they'd be great in bed. There'd been a pull so strong he'd forgotten that sleeping with an employee was a bad idea.

Was this Jenny all over again?

Lord, he would not let that happen.

He took a step back. "Good night."

She smiled one more time, then turned away, off to her bedroom on the third floor, the one right beside his son.

His son.

Crazy feelings fluttered through him. Fear mostly.

He picked up the remote for one of the TVs but dropped it again and walked to his office. He found the number for the private investigator whom his best friend and lawyer Brad had hired to combat his wife's allegations when she'd filed for divorce.

The investigator answered after three rings. "Hello."

"Charlie?"

"Well, as I live and breathe. Grant Laningham. Somebody told me you were dead."

"You should have investigated further. I'm not even hiding."

"You don't call being on an island by yourself hiding?"

Grant laughed. "So, you do keep tabs on me."

"I wouldn't say that I keep tabs. I just like to know where all my people are. What's up?"

"The usual confidentiality applies?"

"Absolutely. I still have that non-disclosure agreement we signed."

"I have a son."

Charlie's voice filled with concern. "Oh."

"His mom died."

Charlie groaned. "Nothing is ever normal with you, is it, Laningham? Seems like when it rains in your life, it pours."

"That's it exactly. But at least this time I'm not having trouble in threes."

"How did you find out about the child?"

"A lawyer brought Max here today along with a copy of his mom's Last Will and Testament and a letter she'd begun writing to explain things. She didn't finish it. But what she'd written ends with her talking about relatives in France, people my son knows."

"You don't have their names?"

"Nope. Don't have their names." He picked up Samantha's letter, glanced at it one more time to be sure he hadn't missed something. "Max's mother is Samantha Baxter. She was a lawyer in Manhattan." He rattled off the name of her law firm. "She should be easy to find. I assume you can locate her relatives once you research her family tree."

Charlie snorted. "Probably. If not, I have my ways. I'll get back to you."

Grant expected to be relieved when he hung up the phone, but he wasn't. He knew he was a little more attracted than he should to his ghostwriter, a woman who out of necessity had to be off-limits because his autobiography had to be above reproach. Now, he was also worried about Max. His son deserved so much better than a workaholic genius for his only family.

He hoped Charlie could quickly find Samantha's cousins.

CHAPTER FOUR

THE NEXT MORNING, Lola made her way downstairs to the front foyer, following the scent of bacon to the dining room where breakfast was already in progress. Grant sat at the head of the eight-person table where they'd had dinner the night before. Max sat on the seat to his right.

"Hey, sleepyhead," Grant said, and Max smiled sheepishly.

The sight of Max smiling mixed with the silly way Grant had greeted her, and Lola had to stop to take it all in. First, Max was here, in the dining room. Grant had to have brought him downstairs. Had he gone to his room to check on him? If he had, that was an extremely responsible thing to do.

Second, the little boy was dressed in shorts and a T-shirt.

Third, Max was smiling. Maybe not full-on grinning. But some of the fear had disappeared from his eyes.

A lump formed in her throat. After the undoubtedly scary time Max had had the day before, the sight of him adjusting almost made her weep.

Grant said, "We had pancakes yesterday so we're having oatmeal and bacon today."

She walked to the empty chair beside Grant. "I like oatmeal."

"We also discovered that Caroline has a grandson Max's age."

"Oh?"

"Yes. She went home to get him so he and Max can swim together this morning, while you and I work."

Words failed her. Then she wondered why. Grant Laningham was one of the smartest people on the planet. He was also a problem solver. He hadn't lost his skills or abilities because the monkey wrench in his plans was a small child not a line of computer code. He did what he did best. He figured things out.

And in such a way that Max wasn't afraid anymore.

That's what surprised her. Not that Grant had solved a problem, but that this man who was usually a bull in a china shop was so sensitive to Max.

Feelings she'd had for him the night before resurrected. The moonlight had combined with the simple, easy way he'd begun relating his story to her and she'd felt she was talking to the real Grant. The guy who lived deep down inside him.

The guy Giovanni knew well enough to decide that the truth of his life would save him from accusations made in his former employee's book.

The real Grant was a nice guy with an unhappy childhood. He was someone who'd made something of himself with hard work and determination. He'd spoken kindly to Max. And was being even nicer to him now.

That was the Grant she had to show in his autobiography.

A woman in a pink uniform brought Lola a bowl of oatmeal. "Thank you."

"This is Denise. She's the cook," Grant said. "Denise, this is Lola. She'll be here six weeks while we work on a project together."

Denise said, "It's nice to meet you."

Lola smiled. "It's nice to meet you too."

"After breakfast Max and I are going to take a walk down the beach, looking for seashells. By the time we return, Caroline should be back. She's going to watch the boys swim, then you and I can get down to business."

She nodded her agreement, no longer surprised but absolutely impressed by his managerial skills. If he kept up this openness and kindness, writing his autobiography would be a breeze.

Sort of.

He didn't want Max to be mentioned in the book.

He also had a history of ending careers.

She herself had witnessed a bit of his temper.

Somehow, she would have to find that thread of goodness inside him and tug on it until she could connect all the things in his life in such a way that they made sense of his actions.

As she added sugar and cinnamon to her oatmeal, Grant said, "I know last night's interview was informal, but shouldn't you be taking notes or maybe recording our sessions?"

She nodded then took a bite of her oatmeal. "Oh, God, that's good."

"Denise is a world-class chef. She hated the cutthroat nature of Michelin starred restaurants. So, I scooped her up. She and her family love South Carolina and she only works three days a week."

"What do you eat the rest of the time?"

"Believe it or not, I'm good on the grill. Plus, some days are sandwich days."

Max gazed at Grant with a combination of curiosity and awe, and she couldn't imagine what would go through a little boy's head as he interacted so casually with a father he hadn't met until the day before.

When Max said, "And some days are takeout days," Lola laughed. She imagined a busy attorney in Manhattan had served takeout a lot. Max was connecting his past life to his new life.

That was a good sign.

Grant said, "Exactly. Though getting takeout

on an island is a little more complicated than it is in Manhattan."

Max studied him for a second. "Do you live at the beach all the time?"

"I have for the past four years. But I may decide to move sometime soon…like in the next couple of months."

Because he was re-entering the business world.

"Where to?" Max asked.

"Well, if I leave here, it will be to go to work. Finding sufficient qualified employees has to factor into the place I choose."

Max nodded.

Grant waited a beat, probably to be sure Max's questions were done, then he addressed Lola again. "So, are we recording our sessions, or do you just take notes?"

"I record *and* take notes. The recording is a backup in case I feel my notes are too loose. But I also use the recordings to verify everything I write."

"What happens to the recordings after we're done?"

"Once you approve the book, you will sign a statement that you said everything that's in the book, and you won't publicly contradict it or sue me because you changed your mind about something. After that, you get the recordings. Destroy them if you like. Or keep them in case something comes up. Most people destroy them."

"Makes sense."

"This isn't my first rodeo. I know how to protect us both."

"Okay."

Caroline entered the room with a little boy whose dark hair looked like someone had put a bowl on his head and cut around it.

"We're back," Caroline said. "This is Jeremy. Jeremy, that's Max."

Max said, "Hi."

Jeremy grinned. "Grammy says you have a dog."

"Benjamin Franklin," Max replied before Grant could. His beach walk with his dad forgotten, he got off his chair. "I'm going to put my bathing suit on."

Jeremy said, "I'll come with you."

The two little boys scrambled out of the room.

Grant chuckled. "Apparently, a love of swimming has already bonded them."

Caroline displayed a bottle of sunblock. "I brought this too. Max is a little fair."

"Good. Maybe you could make a list of things I should have around the house for a little boy?"

"I'll do that while they're swimming." She headed for the door in the back of the dining room. "You two have fun working while I sit by the pool." Her laughter followed her out of the room.

"Watching two kids play would not be a day off for me," Grant said, rising from the table. "But Caroline was thrilled with the idea."

"Grandmothers really love their grandkids."

"That's what it seems." He pushed his chair under the table. "I'll see you in the office in about twenty minutes?"

Lola nodded. "Okay."

As he left, the strangest feeling rumbled through her. She really liked him. She wanted to believe that this was the real Grant Laningham. But she couldn't be fooled. She had to work with him. No, she had to write an accurate depiction of his life. This nice guy had shown up for Max. And only Max.

The real Grant Laningham had almost kissed her the night before.

And she would have let him. There was no denying there was a spark of something between them. Plus, the night had been beautiful. Their conversation had been fun. For a few seconds, she'd wished she wasn't working for him. But that notion fled quickly. A fling might be exciting, but they'd never have anything permanent. He was not the kind of guy that she wanted permanently. Now that her parents had been gone four years, her grief had morphed into loneliness. It was time to rebuild her life. A fling with a crazy narcissist was not the way to do that. Especially if their attraction ruined their ability to work together.

That was what she had to remember when tempted to follow the feelings she had around him. Not only would a relationship between them be unprofessional and risky, but a relationship—even a friendship—with the man she was writing about could skew her perspective.

This was the highest paying job she'd had to date. She had to do it right.

She also had to protect her heart. She had to acknowledge that self-absorbed Grant Laningham could hurt her. Affairs might be a part of normal people's lives, but vulnerable people fell in love too hard, too fast. Even when they knew their partner was all wrong for them. She had enough trouble, loneliness and emptiness. She couldn't risk making all that worse when she was finally at a point where she might be able to let go of her grief and rebuild her life.

Grant strode to his office shaking his head. Lola had dressed appropriately for an island in shorts and a T-shirt but seeing her so casual and comfortable at his dining table had brought back all those wonderful feelings from the night before.

Which was ridiculous. She was a professional here to ghostwrite his autobiography. He had a son, whose life he had to sort out at some point. He couldn't keep Max here if the little boy was supposed to be in Paris, being raised by relatives who knew and loved him. He also had to work on the book, approve everything Lola wrote, guide the process so he accomplished his goals in putting out the story of his life.

He didn't have time to be attracted to her.

They didn't have time for a fling.

He entered his office, walked to the window behind the desk and opened the drapes to expose the amazing view of the ocean. As he was pulling a notebook from his big, mahogany desk, Lola arrived.

She waved a small device at him—probably her recorder. "Ready?"

"Ready." This was exactly what they needed. No more conversations in the moonlight that made him feel like he was talking to a friend. It was time for structure. Recorders. Tablets for taking notes. Conversations about facts.

He *was* ready. More ready than she would ever know.

She sat, placing her notebook and recorder on the desk. "Don't let the recorder intimidate you. I want you to talk the way you did last night. Open. Honest. Casual."

There was no way in hell he would do that. Open, honest, casual had led to inappropriate feelings. Today was the day he took control. He was stronger than any attraction. But he was also smart enough to figure out that part of the lure of her was the simple, easy way she communicated. Today he would do most of the talking. He would direct the conversation.

"I think we should start with my last year at university."

She nodded and motioned for him to begin talking as she pressed the button on her recorder.

He took a breath. "My last year of university I knew I wanted to work for the biggest software developer in the world—"

He went on to describe his friends, their majors and goals, the brainstorming sessions and wishful thinking sessions where he admitted he wanted to best everybody currently working in the tech industry. His friends had laughed and talked about working for him—

"But none of your friends ever worked for you."

"No. They found niches that they liked. For them 'purpose' had a different meaning than it had for me. While I wanted to be the one running the show, they found fulfillment other ways."

Somehow or another that segued into him telling Lola stories of his friends coming to the island for fishing trips. Brad and Matthew, his two best friends, had helped him buy the island when he was still in the hospital after his accident four years ago. They'd taken off work to set up the house and bring the physical therapists in. Brad, a lawyer, had slapped a defamation suit on his wife who had filed for divorce the week before he was hit by the car. The divorce had been inevitable. But he'd objected to letting the end of their marriage play out in the press.

The defamation suit had stopped all her interviews and resulted in a much smaller settlement than he'd thought he'd be handing over to her.

"Interesting."

Jarred out of his reminiscence, he said, "What?"

"You almost died, and she still crucified you in the press."

"Until Brad sued her." He shook his head. "You know what's funny? She'd filed for divorce only days before my accident. Had she waited one week, and I'd been killed, she'd have gotten everything."

"That's morbid."

"No. That's what happens when you get divorced. The good things about our marriage were over after eighteen months. She started traveling. Never being around." He shook his head. "She spent six months in Italy once. I surprised her with a visit and found her lover living in my villa with her."

She grimaced. "And that didn't end your marriage?"

He tilted his head as he thought about how to explain that. "I could give you the easy answer—I was busy creating a new software platform and didn't have time to deal with personal things. And that would be the truth. Except there was a part of me that didn't *want* to deal with it."

"You thought you could fix your marriage?"

"No. Honestly? I believed that's what marriage

was. Two people who stuck together even though they didn't like each other anymore."

She stared at him. "See, right now…as an interviewer… I'm wondering if your parents' marriage taught you that."

"It did. Why do you think they spent so much time apart?"

"They were extremely busy people?"

"With more than just work and altruism."

He watched her face as she made sense of what he'd said.

"Your parents had affairs?"

"Yes."

"So, you didn't see your wife's affairs as being unusual?"

"Money gives people options and opportunities."

"Okay."

He snorted. "I suppose you're going to tell me your parents never strayed."

"They didn't."

"And you would know?"

"Yes. They were hopelessly in love. But also, we lived in a small town. Secrets didn't stay secrets long. Plus, my parents were sort of broke. Not penniless, but—you know—they only had enough money to pay the bills and save a bit here and there."

"You're saying they didn't have the cash for a no-tell motel."

She laughed. "No options. No opportunities.

But don't dismiss the fact that they were crazy about each other. They would slow dance in the kitchen while their chicken and dumpling soup cooked."

"And you think *that's* normal?"

She sighed. "Yes and no."

"You're a dreamer."

"Don't say that like it's a sin!"

"It's not a sin. It just makes life harder."

"Says the guy who admittedly planned his future with his friends long before he even graduated university."

"That was different. I was dealing with facts. I was smart. I was imaginative. I was getting an education. I knew that when I got out into the world there would be no stopping me."

She studied him. "Interesting."

He sighed. "What is *interesting* now?"

"You split hairs. My parents' happy marriage is wishful thinking to you but you *changing the entire world* was just par for the course."

"I had variables that added up. Intelligence, imagination, education," he said, counting off on his fingers. "I was a good pony to put your money on. What did they have? An unreliable emotion?"

"Yes. Except—"

"No *except*. That's all they had."

She frowned and he knew she wanted to argue. Instead, she guided him back to talking about graduating, getting his first job, looking for his place in the industry he wanted to rule.

They paused once when Denise brought a pot of coffee into the office. After that he talked until Denise came in at one o'clock, asking what they wanted for lunch.

He suggested that he grill hot dogs since he had two hungry boys to fill, and Denise left to get everything ready.

Lola turned off her recorder and closed her notebook. "You just spent hours talking virtually nonstop. That's a lot for me to process. I'll be spending the afternoon making notes that will ultimately become an outline."

"I'm not sure what to do with Max this afternoon."

"After a morning of playing in a pool, he might need a nap."

"I'll give him that option. If he declines, I'll probably take him out on the boat for a while."

She gasped. "I'll bet he'll love that."

"One of these days, I want to take him fishing."

"He'll love that too."

Organizing papers on his desk, he casually said, "We need to get that in because I don't know how long he'll be here."

"Excuse me?"

"He's got other family. What if they come looking for him? What if his cousins pop in one day and he's thrilled to see them? He might not want me anymore."

He could see from her expression that she hadn't thought of that, and the idea did not please her.

"We have to have an open mind, Lola. I won't keep him from people who love him and whom he loves."

"You shouldn't. But you should still have a relationship with him."

"I own three jets. A trip to Paris once a month would not be a hardship."

"If he stays here long enough, it won't be that easy for you to give him up."

He sighed. "He is my son. I will never give him up. But I am a realist about my life. He might not fit. He might not *want* to fit."

CHAPTER FIVE

LOLA DECLINED LUNCH. Not only was she not hungry, but she had to get to work. She needed to process everything that had happened that morning.

She'd been worried that she found Grant too attractive and that the good side he was showing might skew her perspective, until he'd started talking about his parents.

She knew people had affairs. She also knew ambition blinded people, so they didn't think what they were doing was wrong. And maybe it wasn't. It sounded like his mom and dad were equal opportunity cheaters. They might have even had an open marriage.

But she'd never thought about how that lifestyle could affect a child. Grant had grown up in a very different world than she had. He saw marriage as something so bleak she wasn't even sure he could define what he thought marriage was.

In a way, she felt sorry for him. She knew the world ran on emotion and connections. Since her parents' deaths she'd seen just how important those things were. Celebrating holidays. Having people to confide in. Knowing people had your back—

She supposed he had those things with his two best friends. Before she'd moved to Montana, she'd had those things with friends, too, but she wanted family. No. She longed for family. For those wonderful ties that had been snatched from her when she'd lost her parents.

With his thoughts on relationships abundantly clear, she no longer had to worry about being attracted to him.

And she had work to do.

She took her notes from that morning's session to the deck outside the bifold panel doors of her bedroom. The thing stretched the length of the house and was filled with Adirondack chairs, chaise lounges, a table and chairs and a hammock. It also had a view of the ocean that took her breath away.

Setting her notes on the table, along with her laptop, she made herself comfortable on one of the chairs.

The scent of grilling hot dogs wafted to her and then evaporated as she read her notes again and again, unable to come up with a theme or a structure for how to showcase Grant's life. The obvious course of the story would be to demonstrate how Max had changed him. But Grant didn't want that. He also might lose Max to Samantha Baxter's extended family. Which was too complicated to sort out in a way that didn't bring his motives into question.

She had to think fresh, think outside the box, figure out how to tell this story.

She toyed with the idea of highlighting the idealistic kid he'd been at university, but lots of people were idealistic before they got into the real world. God knows she had been. Plus, his assessment that he had intelligence, imagination, and an education could come off as vain. Vanity was one of those attitudes they were steering clear of.

No more ideas came. Eventually, she found herself staring at the ocean, thinking again about how different her childhood and Grant's had been.

Her parents had taken her everywhere. Movies. Museums. Theme parks. Zoos. Even to Virginia Beach for vacations. Grant never mentioned a vacation, trip to the zoo, or even a movie.

She didn't want to make his parents out to be negligent, neglectful or even simply bad. Not to protect them, but because that wasn't the tone they wanted to set. Grant was self-made, true. But ruining his parents to demonstrate why he was self-made fed into the he-only-thinks-of-himself attitude most people already had of him, an assumption his book needed to change.

She thought again of her parents. How fun they had been. How easy it had been to return home after trips to war zones or anywhere the global stories were happening.

As if the memories were falling dominoes, she saw the places she'd been, her trips home, and flying off again to cover something significant happening in a distant land. She had been in Kuwait the day she'd gotten the call from her boss to return to New York because her mom and dad had been murdered. Mary Louise Torino, the show's executive producer, had wanted to go to Pennsylvania with her, but Lola had flown into Pittsburgh airport, not JFK. She'd driven to her hometown. Gone to the police station. And crumbled.

The sound of someone knocking on her door came through the opening that led from her suite to the deck. She rose and went back inside to answer the door.

Grant stood in the hall, wincing. "I hate to bother you, but Max is spending some quiet time in his room. If we want to get a little more work done today, we could."

Rather than continue to try to decipher notes that weren't coughing up a theme, time with Grant to get more information might be a better use of the afternoon. "I'll be right down."

He peered into her face. "Are you okay?"

She batted her hand. "Sure. I'm fine. I was just organizing my notes on the deck, and I lost track of time."

"Okay."

She smiled. "Okay."

Closing her suite door, she decided it had to be the smell of the ocean, the reminder of those summer vacations in her teen years that had brought her parents so vividly to her mind. Then she grabbed her notebook and her recorder and returned to Grant's office.

As she sat on the chair across the desk from him, he asked, "So where were we?"

"You'd been talking about school and your friends. But I'm having trouble drilling down to the theme we want for your story or the big picture we want to convey. I thought maybe if we talked in broad strokes for a bit, I could get more of a general idea of who you are. Basically, what I want to be able to do is write an outline that focuses on sections of your life. For instance, school will segue into your first job which will segue into you leaving that company and starting your own company, etc. etc. And from those broad strokes maybe a theme will appear."

"Okay."

He spent the next hour basically outlining his life.

School.
First job.
Left to create apps.
Market too crowded.
Developed new office admin software.

Sales shot to the moon.
Got married.
*Sued by the first company he worked at—
won the suit because his software was not
at all like theirs.*
*Their suit actually advertised why his prod-
uct was better. Sales went through the roof
again.*
*Initial public offering of stock in his com-
pany made him richer than he'd ever imag-
ined possible.*
*Created all kinds of products that made his
shareholders rich.*
Wife had affairs.
His board wanted to play it safe.
He was frustrated.
Angry.
He fired thirty people in thirty days.
Board ousts him.
Wife files for divorce.
Car almost kills him.

"And here we are."

"You don't want to talk about rehab?"

"I told you my friends helped me find this island. I bought it. I did my rehab here."

"Was it difficult?"

He stared at her. "Of course, it was difficult!
And painful."

"Yet you did it because…"

"Because that's how a body heals."

She paused for a second, processing everything. "Looking at the broad strokes, I'd say the theme of your life is that you did what you had to do."

"Always." An odd relief filled his voice. "I always just take the next logical step."

Suspicion fluttered through her. The reporter in her knew he was either hiding something or he felt a little guilty because all the kindness he was showing Max was simply the next step for him. He had no feelings. No love. No empathy for his son. He was merely taking the next step.

Was that why he didn't seem fazed that he might lose his son?

She shook her head to clear it. It didn't matter. He would either raise Max or Max would be raised in France. It would work out.

And Grant would adjust.

His dealings with Max were none of her business—

A thought struck her and she almost gasped. Even if she took Max out of the equation, Grant's life was still changing. He was leaving his island and returning to work. Whether he knew it or not, to ease his way back into the business world, he would have to be a better person.

She suspected Giovanni knew that. Gio might have insisted on this autobiography to help Grant see that he couldn't hire an office full of staff and fire half of them the way he had the former employees who hated him.

He had to change.

And the universe had sent him Max.

She'd already seen a kinder, nicer side of Grant because of Max.

She might not be able to put Max into the biography, but she couldn't help noticing that Grant was changing.

Taking the next step, the way he always did.

She returned to her suite to input the broad strokes of his life into her computer, almost as an outline. The theme of change, Grant changing, really grew on her. She could set up his life, show where he had gone wrong, demonstrate that he knew he had to change to go back to work with a new company, a new staff, new investors and a new board.

And maybe even end it on a cliffhanger: a *Will he change? Will he make it?* ending.

It wasn't the perfect idea yet, but something about it felt like she was on the right track. She knew from experience that stories frequently twisted and turned. Themes morphed.

But for now, she had a vision of a sort, something that could guide her into asking the right questions.

She felt so good about it that she showered and dressed for dinner in a sundress and flip-flops. She let her humidity-curly hair go wild and crazy and went downstairs to the patio by the pool where Grant was again grilling.

When she saw only Max lounging on a chaise with one of his chapter books, and Grant manning the grill, she stopped. "Did Jeremy go home?"

"After lunch, remember?"

That was right. He'd gone home after the hot dogs, when Max had gone upstairs, maybe not to nap, but to rest a bit. The second work session that afternoon had made it feel like two days instead of one. That's why she'd gotten confused.

Max pulled his sunglasses down his nose so he could look at her. "He's coming back tomorrow."

She didn't know where Max had gotten sunglasses, but he was clearly enjoying the beach lifestyle.

"That's cool."

Grant agreed. "He'll be back tomorrow morning for swimming and palling around while we work." Grant snorted. "Getting to kid-watch by the pool has Caroline acting like she's died and has gone to heaven."

Lola laughed.

"Then while you assemble your notes in the afternoon, I'm taking the boys out on the boat."

She glanced at Max. "Wow. That sounds fun."

Max nodded. "It's going to be awesome."

She looked for signs that Max was upset and saw none. Whatever Grant was telling him behind closed doors, it was helping him to cope.

As she walked over to the grill, Grant gave her a quick once-over. "You look nice."

His unexpected compliment sent a ripple of pleasure through her. "Yeah. The book's starting to come together in my head, so I thought I'd dress up to celebrate." She glanced at the steaks on the grill. "Anything I can do to help?"

Grant leaned against the sideboard and crossed his arms on his chest. "No. Just got to wait for everything to cook. We're good." He nodded toward the table. "Max and I even set the table."

She smiled approvingly as she glanced at it. Grant was absolutely changing. She wouldn't mention it and mess it up, but right now the theme of Grant changing seemed to be right on the money.

Max said, "I used to set the table all the time."

"We also talked about his mom a bit more," Grant said, giving her a significant look.

Realizing she was correct, Grant was talking to Max, helping him to deal with the loss of his mother when they were alone, she glanced at the little boy who had gone back to reading.

"Yeah. They didn't have a memorial service. So, I called Fletcher. We're going to have one."

She peeked at Max again. He was still fine. "Here?"

"We decided on Manhattan. You know...a day trip on a private jet. That way we can sort of... Wrap it all up."

He was talking about giving Max closure.

Those conversations he was having with his son weren't a one-way street. Grant really was listening to Max, thinking things through, doing what Max needed. It was simultaneously smart and sweet. Max wasn't just a logical next step. Grant was being a father to him.

Her heart warmed as she said, "Okay. I can use the day you're gone to work on the book."

"You're on the guest list."

She blinked. "There's a guest list?"

"Yes. Fletcher gave me some names. I have a private detective looking for Samantha's cousins so they can be invited too. It'll be small. Late Friday morning." He flipped the steaks. "I thought we'd need a break from the book anyway. Plus, there are still things belonging to Max in Samantha's condo. We need to get them out before it's handed over to a real estate agent."

She nodded, once again peeking over at Max. If he was paying attention to their conversation, he was okay with it. Probably because Grant had already talked all this through with him.

They ate their steaks with salads and finished the cherry pie Denise had made the day before. After dinner, Max sat with his feet in the pool, with Benjamin Franklin at his side. The whole evening had been subdued. Grant might be helping Max, but the little boy still silently grieved. Even the dog appeared to be making sure Max was okay.

She let Grant put Max to bed on his own and was just about to leave the pool patio and go to her room when he returned. "He has a million questions."

"I'll bet."

He retrieved two beers from the outdoor kitchen refrigerator. "Luckily, I had read a few articles on children grieving."

She took the beer he handed her. "When did you have time?"

"After lunch before I came to your room to get you, I searched the internet."

"And?"

"And it appears that when talking to a child about death, honesty is the best policy."

"It usually is."

"When he came downstairs, I asked him if he had any questions, and he did."

"And you helped him?"

"You say that as if it astounds you."

"No. It's all good." It was better than good. He didn't merely have instincts; he had worked Max into his life. He made concessions. He gave Max the kind of priority Lola would bet he never gave anyone else.

Even though she was seeing it, it still amazed her. She couldn't forget this was the guy who'd fired someone every day for a month. After he told a reporter he'd done it to motivate them, most people believed he couldn't possibly have any empathy to indiscriminately fire thirty people with families and mortgages.

But after his accident and with his son, Grant seemed to be behaving like an entirely different person. The theme of Grant changing solidified in her brain.

Grant said, "What fell together for you today about the book?"

"The idea that you're a guy who takes the next logical step," she said, careful to keep the word *change* out of her answer for two reasons. First, she didn't want to influence him. If the book was about change, the theme would happen naturally. Second, he might not like the idea that he was changing. She was seeing it, but he might not be. She didn't want to inadvertently tamper with that.

"You have goals and smarts. But you also have a nice thread of logic that runs through your life—evidenced by how you're handling Max."

He laughed. "It always amazes me when someone assumes logic is unusual. You do realize there was a time when the world ran on logic."

"Not so much anymore." She took a pull on her beer. "Everybody's out for the next big thing, instead of the next logical step."

"Exactly."

The ocean breeze wafted over to them. She inhaled deeply. "It's so peaceful here."

"It is." He glanced around. "This might sound

weird, but the place feels totally different with Max here."

"I'll bet your pool never got so much use."

He laughed. "My dog has also never had so much fun."

"You'll miss him if he leaves to live in France."

"Maybe. But I also don't want to do the wrong thing. God only knows what will happen when I go back to work. I barely have time for sleep, let alone time for a little boy. Plus, he could *choose* to live with his French cousins. I don't want him to feel pressured."

He also didn't want to be disappointed. He didn't say it. But up to this point he'd been leaning toward *wanting* Max to be raised by people he knew. Now that Grant himself was someone Max knew, he'd included himself in the equation.

All these changes gave her reason to hope that he wouldn't just shuffle Max off to a new home while he was still grieving, still trying to find his way. Grant was going to do the right thing for his little boy.

She laughed, suddenly feeling a million pounds lighter. Max would be cared for. Her book had found its legs. She could stop worrying.

The silent night air relaxed her a little more.

"So how many ghostwriting projects have you done?"

She looked over at Grant, not surprised he'd

changed the subject. "Only four. One a year since I bought the ranch."

He gaped at her. "You bought that ranch immediately after your parents died?"

"I went through some horrific emotions. Made worse by the fact that they caught the guys who killed my parents almost immediately. They were two addicts looking for money for drugs. My dad apparently heard them and came out to the kitchen. The one kid panicked and shot him. My mom raced out and they shot her."

"Oh, my God. I'm sorry."

"The kids were caught just down the street. The evidence against them was overwhelming. They still had the gun on them. Had my dad's wallet. They confessed, told the story of my parents coming into the kitchen, then took a plea deal to avoid the death penalty. And it was done."

He studied her for a second. "That quick?"

"Yes. It was set in stone in less than a week."

"That must have been jarring."

"That's exactly the word for it. My parents were gone—never coming back. I felt like there should have been more to it than that. You know…some time at least to process things."

She took a breath. "Instead, I was left feeling out of sorts and unable to get myself back to normal. I tried returning to work, even flew to New York but couldn't leave the airport to go to the office. I'd broken an engagement to take the assignment of traveling for the network. I'd given up the love of my life for a job—"

"You'd given up the love of your life?"

"I was engaged when I got the network job offer. Jeff was a happy small-town guy, homespun." She smiled. "He reminded me of my dad. When I got the offer, the whole world opened up to me and I knew I couldn't refuse it. It was everything I'd studied for. Everything I secretly dreamed about. But I also knew Jeff couldn't handle having the mother of his kids in a war zone. That would not have been fair to him. So, I broke off our engagement."

"Sounds like a no-win situation."

"It was."

"Did you miss him?"

"I didn't at first. The job was everything I wanted and more." She shook her head. "I can't even explain how happy I was. And he found somebody else. I totally believed I'd made the right choice. Then my parents were killed, and the reality of life set in. The job might have been wonderful, but I didn't have a close friend who wasn't connected to the network. I also didn't have a partner. Or a home anymore. Without my parents, there was no home. When I most needed someone in my life, I was alone."

"Like Max is now."

Two days ago, his perception would have surprised her. Today, she realized he saw everything, processed everything, around him. Maybe even with more understanding than a true narcissist would have. Meaning, he might not actually be a narcissist, but simply an exacting businessman, so focused on his work he always did what he believed needed to be done—damn the consequences.

"My parents were gone. The job I'd ditched the man I loved for was suddenly irrelevant. Pointless. My life was a big, black hole and it seemed that every major choice I'd made had been wrong."

"I felt that when I woke up in the hospital."

His perception might not surprise her, but his admission had. "Oh, yeah?"

He chuckled. "Oh, yeah. I built a company that a board of directors could yank out from under me when they decided my management style was inappropriate. I'd married a woman I no longer even liked most days. And some fool on his phone almost killed me. I was like…what's the point?"

"My realization was more like there's got to be more to life than this. Or maybe there has to be a way to blend what I needed personally with what I needed professionally."

"So how did you end up with a ranch?"

"I rented a car at the airport and started to drive. After a week of hotels and fast food I found myself in Montana. Where I was reminded of nothing. I knew no one. Nothing reminded me of the love I'd pointlessly thrown away. I hadn't done a story anywhere west of the Mississippi. None of that was even vaguely familiar. And, honestly, it was a relief to feel nothing. The house was quaint. Most of the time my world was silent. I found peace and after the first year of grief, I felt better. Then the reality of the finances kicked in."

He nodded, which she took as permission to keep talking.

"I should have rented a house in peaceful, quiet Montana…or even *bought* a house. Instead, I'd bought a *ranch*."

"And now you're broke?"

"And now I'm broke. The place doesn't make money. It *costs* money. The cattle I sell only pays for the hands who work there, and part of the feed. Every cent I've earned ghostwriting goes into that money pit. Most of my retirement is gone because I need it now. If I don't do something soon, I will have to file for bankruptcy."

"Why don't you sell it?"

"It's beginning to look like that's my only option. I gave running the place my best shot. I can't make it profitable. Once we finish your book, I'll meet with a real estate agent. I'll probably take a loss…which essentially will mean ponying up the rest of my savings. But I'll be free."

"And then what?"

She shrugged. "This ghostwriting gig is pretty fun."

He laughed. "That can't be a living."

"It pays better than you think. Plus, I still have my parents' house in Pennsylvania."

His eyebrows rose. "After four years?"

"I rented it out."

"Ah."

"I should probably make a decision about that. You know…get some closure for myself."

"From what I read, closure is the thing. You can't go forward until you make peace with the loss by tying up loose ends."

"Those must have been some articles you read."

He laughed. "They were. That's the brilliance of the internet. You really can find just about anything you need to know."

He leaned back on his chair, linking his hands behind his neck. The material of his T-shirt stretched across his muscular chest, drawing her eyes to it. Attraction twinkled through her. Urges she hadn't felt in forever blossomed. She hadn't even been held by a man in four long years. The time had flown, and she had barely been aware of it. But being with Grant seemed to be waking up the part of her she'd forgotten existed.

"The danger is not checking and rechecking the information, verifying sources."

She took a quiet breath. *His* waking up her hormones was one thing. *Her* acting on her reactions was quite another. Even as attractive as he was, he wasn't her type. She liked stable, quiet, happy people. Her ex had been the epitome of the strong, silent type. A guy who wanted a family and a home in a small town like her parents'. She wasn't sure that was what she wanted now. But she'd never forgotten how happy she had been with Jeff. All because his strength came from stability. After losing everything, she now knew the importance of that.

Grant's emotions were all over the board and usually confusing. Worse, his beliefs about relationships were opposite hers.

She did not need to worry about or even pay attention to her awakening hormones. He was not the right guy for her.

"Look who you're talking to. I was on network news. Verifying was my middle name."

The night got quiet again. The peace she'd felt before returned, surrounding her like a blanket. The decision to sell the ranch was the first step to finding her way back to herself. Her real self. Then maybe she'd be ready to look for love again.

She could give Grant a little credit for the decisions that were coming so easily tonight, but only because he owned the island where her stalled-out brain seemed to be clearing. He was the first person who'd gotten her to talk about her parents, about the ranch, because in a way she knew that part of her story reflected poorly on her. Even though she'd needed the peace and quiet of Montana, the answer hadn't been to buy a business she couldn't run. Most people would see that as at least bad judgment. Others might think she'd taken a tumble off the deep end.

It had been easy to tell him, though. Not only did he understand mistakes because he'd made some whoppers, but also he was smart enough not to judge but to listen—

She saw it then. The danger. She was a serious person who wanted to mend her life. And here she was on a private island with a handsome man, somebody she found incredibly attractive, somebody she was easily opening up to. If she didn't watch herself, something could happen between them. While his good looks and charm drew her, telling her story, connecting with someone after years of being alone, was a hundred times more tempting.

Especially since she was coming out of her grief, ready to be herself again and most likely vulnerable.

She had to put some distance between them.

She rose from the patio table. "I should turn in."

He smiled at her. "Me too. I'll see you in the morning."

Her chest tightened. Sharing with him had seemed objective, but his smile was warm with intimacy. He kept saying she'd witnessed the oddest moment of his life. Now, he knew she'd screwed up royally after her parents' deaths.

They had a connection.

He rose out of politeness but that put them toe-to-toe again, as they'd been on the first night she'd stayed here—the night she knew he'd considered kissing her. The warm air filled with that kind of promise again, a kiss, a potential romance to satisfy their attraction—

She stopped those thoughts, reminding herself she and Grant were not a good match. Still, as she walked into his house, a house with which she was now familiar, the connection she felt with him strengthened, confusing her.

The sense that she belonged here rippled through her.

But she didn't belong here. She couldn't. Even Grant intended to leave this island to return to work. There was not a place here for her.

She shook her head, telling herself to stop imagining things that weren't there. Particularly those connections she was so sure she felt. They could be nothing. Grant's attraction to her might not be as strong as she thought—

No. A woman always knew when a man wanted to kiss her.

Still, it didn't have to be a problem if she kept her distance with Grant. If she couldn't, she would keep her wits about her and notice when things began turning into something they shouldn't. That was how a person survived in a war zone.

She laughed to herself. She'd been to real war zones. An unwanted attraction did not qualify as one, but the instinct for self-preservation was real and right—

Or maybe it was a sign that *all* her instincts were returning?

That she really was coming back to herself after four long years of grief and confusion.

She stopped on the stairway. She was coming back. That's why she could remember her parents without falling into a deep depression. That's why she was seeing so much into what was happening with Grant. The reporter she had been was finally waking up.

CHAPTER SIX

THE NEXT MORNING at breakfast, Grant waited until Lola arrived before he turned to Max. He didn't necessarily need Lola's support, but he did want her to be apprised of what was going on.

"We have something important to talk about."

Max said, "We do?"

Lola's attention fixed on Grant.

"Your mom gave me a letter that says you are my son. But there are reasons I believe we need to be sure of that." When Max looked confused, Grant said, "Reasons we need to confirm that."

Still confused, Max glanced at Lola.

Which was exactly why he had wanted her in the room. He was good with Max. But every once in a while, he needed backup.

"There's a test," she said. "A DNA test that will tell us for sure that Grant is your dad."

Max's gaze whipped back to Grant.

"It's a precaution."

Lola tapped Max's hand so he would look at her. "We're doing the test to make sure. So that

there aren't complications down the road. But we're
fairly certain you're Grant's son."

Max nodded.

Grant said, "Your mom's letter told me that you
had some cousins in France."

"Mademoiselle Janine and Monsieur Pierre."

Grant didn't know why he was surprised Max
knew their names. Samantha had said they spent
time with them. But the little boy's familiarity
with them shot the oddest negative feeling through
him. Something strong enough to tighten his gut.

"Mademoiselle is a lawyer like Mom was."

The easy way he spoke again struck Grant neg-
atively, but he ignored that in favor of practicality.
Max knowing their names could make Charlie's
job a lot easier. "Do you know their last name?"

"Rochefort."

Denise arrived with bacon and eggs for Grant
and a toasted cheese sandwich for Max. She asked
Lola what she would like, and Lola requested a
bagel and coffee.

Pins and needles raced through Grant. He had
no time or patience for mundane things like breakfast with Max speaking so casually about people
Grant didn't know, but Max appeared to know
very well.

"What does Pierre do?"

"He's a painter," Max said then took a big bite
of his sandwich. "He lets me paint too." He peered
at Grant. "With *oils*."

Lola said, "That sounds fun."

Max turned serious. "Oils are expensive."

Grant frowned. "Oh, do the Rocheforts have money troubles?"

Lola sent Grant a warning look at the insensitive question.

But Max shook his head. "I don't know. They live in a huge house. With a yard as big as the park by our condo where Mom took me to play."

"Oh."

Max ate another three bites of the sandwich in quick succession.

"Anyway," Grant said, "I have a friend who will be coming here this morning to start the test."

Max nodded. He quickly finished his sandwich. "Can I watch cartoons?"

"Sure."

"I'll go with you," Lola said, rising from her seat.

"You haven't gotten your bagel yet."

"I can eat it cold."

Grant heard the subtle recrimination in Lola's voice, but he had absolutely no idea what he'd done wrong. He couldn't have his doctor take the DNA swab without an explanation to Max. He also hadn't thought he was insensitive asking about Pierre and Janine.

Anger skittered through him. He hated their pretentious names—

He stopped himself. Confusing emotions buffeted him. One was fear. He hadn't even known Max three full days, but the thought of handing him over to strangers set his nerve endings on fire. Now, he understood what Lola had been telling him the day Max arrived when she'd said he couldn't hand the little boy over to strangers. But they weren't strangers to Max. They were strangers to Grant—

Who—as his father—was the one charged with protecting him. Even if that meant protecting him from the odd, probably lonely life he'd have with Grant.

The sound of Jason returning on the sea cruiser eased into the dining room. With a sigh, Grant tossed his napkin to the table and walked out of the house toward the dock.

As he reached the boat, his friend, Art Montgomery, the doctor who had cared for him when he arrived on the island to heal, jumped out. Wearing shorts and a tropical print shirt, he shook Grant's hand.

"So how are you feeling?"

"A little overwhelmed." He slapped Art's back. "Getting the DNA results will help a lot."

"I understand. You can't make decisions until you know for sure the little guy is yours."

"Right." He agreed in principle, but he thought of the French cousins and Max running into their arms and his nerves caught fire again. Deciding it had to be because he didn't know the Rocheforts, he made the plan to call Charlie as soon as Art left and have him dig up every piece of information known to mankind on the lawyer and painter, who lived on a property with a yard as big as a park.

Not that he was angry, bitter or jealous. He was just concerned for Max.

Really.

Art caught his arm. "All that's great. But I was talking about your health—your legs. Is everything okay?"

"Yeah. Great. Fine. Wonderful."

"You'd tell me if they weren't."

Grant laughed. "I count on you. So, yes. I would tell you."

They walked to the house and Grant guided Art to follow him in through the family room doors. A set of steps took them to the main floor where Max, Benjamin Franklin and Lola sat on the big leather sofa, watching television, waiting for Jeremy to arrive with Caroline.

"Hey, Max. This is my friend, Art. He's a doctor."

Art smiled at Max.

Max said, "Hi."

"Hi to you too," Art said ambling over to the sofa beside Max.

"That's Lola Evans," Grant said. "She's helping me with a project. Lola, this is Art Montgomery."

"Pleasure to meet you."

"Pleasure to meet you too," Art said, shaking her hand.

The way Art smiled at Lola sent the same weird feelings shooting through him as thinking of Max running into the arms of the French couple.

He reminded himself he couldn't have anything with Lola beyond their work relationship, but he seriously hated the idea of her with another man.

He took a cleansing breath and smiled at Max. "Art's going to take the swab we need to do the DNA test we talked about."

Max nodded.

"There's nothing to be afraid of," Art said. He pulled a swab from his bag and unwrapped it. "In fact, I'll demonstrate on your dad."

Grant nodded and sat on one of the chairs.

Still talking to Max, Art said, "I'm just going to put this in your mouth and swipe it a few times—"

Grant opened his mouth. Art put the swab in and rubbed along his cheek, demonstrating for Max.

"When I'm done, you and old Ben can go out to the pool."

Max nodded again. Lola watched him carefully. Probably looking for signs of distress. Grant appreciated that she was so protective with Max, but right now, in this minute, Grant was filled with more distress than he'd imagined a person could feel.

What would he do if Max *wasn't* his? Send

him to some pretentious people in France? Forget about him?

Why the hell had he even asked for confirmation, when he could have taken Samantha's letter at face value and raised Max himself?

The questions confused him so much his breath stuttered.

Art swabbed the inside of Max's mouth and Max smiled and faced Grant. "Can I get my bathing suit on?"

"Sure," Lola answered before Grant could. "I'll even take you out to the pool, so you'll be there when Jeremy and Caroline get here."

He nodded eagerly and raced off. Art packed up the swab and headed to the door. "If I put a rush on this, we'll have an answer tomorrow."

Grant walked him outside and then to the dock. "Thanks for coming out."

"It's good for me to see you doing so well," Art said, stepping into the boat again. "You made a remarkable recovery."

"And now it's time to go back to work."

Art shook his head. "If I had an island like this, I'd never leave."

"So, what you're saying is I should look for employees willing to work here."

Art laughed and jumped inside the cruiser.

The boat eased away from the dock. Grant returned to the house, but he heard the sound of

Benjamin Franklin and Max in the pool and went to the back patio.

He ambled to the chaise beside the one Lola sat on. "I thought that went okay."

Her gaze never left Max. "Nine-year-olds are tricky. I wasn't sure how much he understood. He's smart enough to know what you were doing, but I don't think he comprehended why. I also recognized you had to be honest with him. But I hope he doesn't start connecting dots and thinking you're trying to get rid of him."

All the horrible feelings Grant had when Max talked about Janine and Pierre rose again like ugly black ghosts in a graveyard. "You heard how he talked about Janine and Pierre. Pierre who lets him paint with *oils*."

Lola studied his face for a few seconds, then she laughed. "You're jealous!"

"Of people I don't know? I don't think so. But I am worried about Max, and I do see what you were saying about not rushing him into going to live with them."

"Are you inviting them to the memorial service?"

"I have a private eye who's worked for me since my divorce. If he finds them, I'll have Fletcher call them to see if they can come to the memorial."

"Makes sense."

"And if they can't, then we have to take a trip to visit them before *any* decisions are made."

She nodded.

He glanced at Max and Benjamin Franklin. "If you want to get set up, I'll wait for Caroline and Jeremy."

She rose from the chaise. "Okay. See you in a few minutes."

Caroline and Jeremy arrived almost immediately after she left. His house manager shooed Grant inside, and he headed to the office where Lola awaited him. He talked about starting his company for what felt like minutes but was actually hours.

Then he took the boys out on the boat that afternoon. But the strangest feeling followed him around all day.

The sense that this child had changed his life without even trying.

New concerns arose. He knew who he was and what he wanted. Could he suddenly change his mind about goals he'd had forever? Not only was that impractical, but also, he had to take Max's needs into consideration. Wouldn't it be better to be raised by a loving couple than a single workaholic dad?

He thought of his sister. The way she could fool babysitters and sneak out of the house. The trouble she got into that his parents never saw. Anything would be better than being raised by a parent who ignored him, left him to his own devices, forced him to figure out life for himself.

He couldn't pay attention to the crazy feelings swelling his heart in his very tight chest. He had to do the right thing. Not for himself, but for Max.

The next day Art called with the news that Max was his son. The relief he felt was overshadowed by truth. He wanted to raise Max. But for once in his life, he could not be selfish. He could not inflict the same kind of mixed-up childhood he'd had on Max.

Still, he also couldn't hand his child over to people he didn't know—

They had to spend time with the Rochefort couple.

Because the most important thing to factor into this decision was Max. It seemed that he loved Janine and Pierre but what if he didn't?

What if he wanted to live with Grant?

Would he change his plans for his future? Could he?

When they boarded Grant's luxurious jet on Friday morning, Lola glanced around in awe. The buttery brown leather seats weren't arranged in rows, but rather seating areas. Four seats in the back could have been a conversation grouping. The four seats in the front were arranged around a small table.

"Why don't you stow that laptop," Grant said, pointing to an overhead compartment in the back. "And play Yahtzee with me and Max."

She looked at Max, adorable in his black suit,

white shirt and little black tie. She longed to give
him anything he wanted, be anything he wanted,
to help make this day go easier. But that was actually part of her problem. It had been too natural
to like Grant, to simply be herself with him, so
she'd decided she had to pull back. But the trip
this morning pointed out that she was also getting too involved with Max and it might be difficult for him when she left.

Though she'd be as present for the sweet little
boy as she could, she also realized the importance
of maintaining some distance to make her leaving
easier on him—the way it should be. She was not
part of the little family they were making. She
was a temporary employee. She was finally seeing how confusing the situation had gotten, but
she could fix it.

She patted her laptop case. "I brought work."

"Yeah, we figured that," Grant said with a
laugh. "But you could take a break."

The urging in his voice tempted her. She'd loved
playing games with her parents as a kid. Her mom
and dad had made her part of everything in their
lives. But she was not really part of Max's life—
or Grant's. She was hired help. She didn't want
Max feeling that he had lost someone else when
she left.

She stowed the laptop for takeoff but sat in one
of the chairs away from the game table. "Don't
forget that we have a deadline."

Grant said, "Okay. Do your thing," but Max's head tilted in question.

She wished Grant would explain to his son that they were working on a book that needed to be completed within a certain time frame. That would go a long way to helping Max understand her position in his life. But Grant said nothing more about her, just retrieved the game from a bin beside his chair.

"We can't play until the plane is in the air," he said to Max. "So, let's buckle up and get this trip started."

Max said, "Okay," but his gaze slid back to her again.

She ignored him, knowing that ten minutes from now when he was engrossed in the game, his confusion would be gone.

The plane took off and reached cruising altitude. Grant set up the Yahtzee game and he and Max began playing.

Lola retrieved her laptop. With no table in the little conversation area, she set it on her lap, which bunched the skirt of her black sheath. She straightened it then slipped off her black pumps to get comfortable for the flight.

Just as her mom had always told her to travel with an umbrella and a raincoat, she'd had Lola pack a little black dress and black pumps no matter where she was going.

"Just in case," she would say.

In the middle of reading her notes from Grant's last two sessions, Lola smiled to herself. Her mother had been a pistol. More than anything, Lola missed her unsolicited advice and folksy wisdom. She also missed her dad's bear hugs. Barbecuing on the back deck in the dead of winter—

Max cried, "Yahtzee!" and Grant groaned.

"You're the luckiest kid I know."

Max giggled but Lola winced at his poor choice of words given that they were flying to his mom's memorial service. Still, she said nothing. There were plenty of times every day when Max and Grant played together or swam together or took walks on the beach without her while she worked. Staying out of their conversation solidified the idea that she was here to do a job.

She took a breath and began arranging notes, turning phrases into sentences and sentences into paragraphs, until the pilot announced that they were landing in twenty minutes and gear should be stowed before they fastened themselves into their seats.

They taxied along the private airstrip to a hangar where a limo awaited them. Max piled in then Grant motioned for Lola to get inside before he slid onto the seat beside Max. She'd deliberately put herself on the bench seat across from them, keeping that little bit of distance, to ease Max away from seeing her as part of their family.

Grant said, "Remember what we talked about last night?"

Max nodded. "I remember."

Lola tried not to notice his serious eyes and somber expression, but the little boy's sorrow couldn't be missed.

"This might be really hard," Grant said.

Max nodded.

"If you want to cry that's okay. If you want to punch something save that for when we get home."

Max nodded again.

Lola stopped a smile. She couldn't imagine Max wanting to punch something, but apparently that was a possibility that Grant and Max had discussed the night before.

That was another thing. Max and Grant had lots of conversations when he put his little boy to bed. She wasn't there for that. And that was what really demonstrated that she wasn't part of their family.

They spent lots of time without her. As long as she maintained this distance, she wouldn't need to worry about Max missing her.

The drive to the mausoleum where Samantha's ashes had already been interred took longer than Lola had anticipated but Max and Grant appeared to be unfazed. Though they didn't speak much, neither seemed nervous. Both were quiet.

They finally arrived. The limo drove by a small line of cars then stopped in front of the building entrance. The driver came around and opened the door. Lola stepped out. Max got out. Grant slid out.

He sucked in a breath, then took Max's hand.

Max smiled up at him.

Lola's chest expanded. Grant had absolutely no idea how attuned he was with his son, but they had nonverbal communication down to a science. More than that, Max trusted Grant. She could see it in his solemn eyes.

They walked into the building and Gio greeted them. Tall with dark hair and green eyes, he said, "Hello," to Lola, squeezed Grant's shoulder in one of those male gestures of solidarity, then he stooped down in front of Max.

"Are you okay?"

Max nodded.

"That's Gio," Grant told Max. "He helped arrange most of this."

Gio smiled. Max nodded again.

Max's silence might have concerned Lola, except he was still communicating, nodding. And looking to Grant.

Gio directed them to the seats in the front row. They passed Fletcher, who waved slightly. The rest of the seats were populated by well-dressed men and women who could have been friends, coworkers or neighbors of Samantha's. There were enough people that they couldn't easily be categorized.

And no one had told her if Janine and Pierre had been found, and if they had been, if they were coming to the memorial service.

A clergyman walked behind the podium and began talking about Samantha. How smart she was. How well liked she was. What a great mom she was.

Max raised his head proudly.

Lola's chest pinched. Her parents had been buried on the same day, the same service, in side-by-side burial plots. The whole town had been there. A lot of her friends from the network had flown down for the funerals.

She'd been numb. She could barely remember what the minister had said about them. She hadn't even had anger to comfort her since the perpetrators had been caught and made a plea deal.

It had been a surreal nightmare.

The service ended. Max slid a rose in the small vase on the door of his mom's interment space. Lola didn't wonder why Samantha had chosen to have her remains put in a mausoleum. Max was too young to be given her ashes and with a place like a mausoleum, if he ever wanted to visit, he would know where to find her.

Samantha, it seemed, had thought of everything.

She must have been a great person.

Lola hoped Max would remember her.

They filed out of the small room. At the door,

Grant and Max accepted condolences. From Max's polite thank-yous, it was clear Grant had coached him. He cried twice and Grant comforted him. To look at them, it was hard to believe they'd only *met* when Fletcher brought him to the island a few days ago.

A gentleman walked up to Max and his eyes widened. "Pierre!"

He stooped down and scooped Max into his arms. *"Mon fils."* He hugged Max tightly. "How are you?"

Max looked at the floor. "I'm okay."

Pierre hugged him again. "I am so sorry." He broke the hug and rose. He extended his hand to Grant. "I'm Pierre Rochefort."

Grant shook his hand. "I'm Grant Laningham."

"Oui. I have read about you. Your ideas are genius."

Lola stood off to the side. She'd seen Grant's eyes narrow when Pierre said he'd read about him. But they returned to normal when he'd called Grant's ideas genius.

"Thank you." He smiled at the man. Slightly older than Grant, Pierre had a few strands of gray in his dark hair. "Would you care to have lunch with us?"

"Actually, I arranged to fly out soon. Janine had a trial, and it was too late to ask for a continuance or for someone else to stand in for her and I need to get home."

"I'm sorry. The memorial was a spur of the moment thing," Grant said. "Max and I were talking, and we decided we needed to do it."

"I understand," Pierre said, perfectly reasonably, like someone who didn't get ruffled easily.

Lola liked him on the spot. She didn't miss the way Max eased over and caught his hand, as if he were accustomed to holding it.

"I miss you," Max said, his voice shaking.

"I miss you too." Pierre stooped to Max's level again. "And we will see you very soon." He hugged Max again. Tears filled his eyes, as he held on tightly, the bond between them evident.

He let Max go and swallowed hard. "My plane leaves in a little over an hour, just enough time to get to the airport." He caught Grant's gaze. "But we have much to discuss."

Grant pulled in a breath. An odd tension passed between them. Grant took Max's hand and eased him beside him. Pierre looked down at Max, obviously seeing the proprietary gesture for what it was.

Grant didn't like Pierre.

Or maybe he'd just gotten his first taste of what losing Max would feel like?

Gio came over. "The superintendent of Samantha's building is waiting for us with the combination to her condo door." As if just noticing Pierre, he said, "I'm sorry. I didn't mean to interrupt. I'm Giovanni, Grant's publicist."

"It's fine. I'm on my way to the airport. It was a pleasure to meet you," he said to Grant.

In all the tension of the situation, everyone had taken their focus off Max. When Lola looked down at him, the little boy was staring at the rose he'd slid into the holder beside his mom's interment spot.

It was as if he'd suddenly realized this was the last moment he'd have of his mom. His little blue eyes filled with tears.

Pierre said, "Goodbye," and headed to the right. Gio directed Grant and Max to the waiting limo. "I have my car. I'll meet you at the building."

Grant said, "Okay."

Lola's eyes ached with the weight of unshed tears. She'd been an adult when she'd lost her parents. Max was nine. He would live most of his life without his mother. She swore she could see that realization in his face. The absolute unfairness of life filled her tired, lonely soul. It had been a long, lost four years for her. Now, Max was facing the same thing.

Holding Max's hand Grant led him back to the limo. Lola silently followed them, her heart heavy. Her emotions about the loneliness she knew Max was about to face mixed with her own loneliness and filled her with sorrow.

Max stopped suddenly. Still holding Grant's hand, he turned to face her. She kept walking until she reached them.

Looking at her through his tears, he caught her hand and started to the limo again. "You should walk with us."

The sweetness of him including her nearly did her in. All this time she'd worried that he would miss her when she was gone when the truth was she would probably miss him more.

When they were seated in the limo, Max slid off the seat with Grant and sat beside her. "It's okay."

Her tears fell. "I know."

Grant wiped away tears too. "We're going to stop at the condo, gather some of Max's things, then make arrangements for the rest to be boxed and shipped to us."

Lola nodded.

"Then we're having a nice lunch before we head home."

Max caught her gaze. "I'm going to be okay."

She smiled through her tears. "Of course, you are. Pretty soon all your memories will be of good things you did with your mom. They'll all be happy."

He nodded. "That's what my dad said."

The proud way he said "my dad" hurt her heart. Grant was taking to parenting like a fish to water, but she'd seen Max catch Pierre's hand. The decision about where Max should live might not be Grant's. Max might actually want to live with Janine and Pierre. What had been Grant's hope when Max first arrived now might be his greatest sorrow.

She was thinking exactly that that night, sitting on Grant's dock, looking out over the dark water that sporadically sparkled in the light of the moon.

"You okay?"

She turned to see Grant standing behind her. She hadn't even heard him approaching.

"Yeah. I'm fine."

Dressed in jeans and a T-shirt, as she was, he lowered himself beside her. "Long day."

"Is Max asleep?"

"Out like a light."

"He adores you."

He looked out over the water. "I love him too. I see myself in him. Tall, skinny, looking around at everything, trying to figure out what's going on. Except he has good reason to be confused. I just had bad parents."

She laughed. "You did okay raising yourself."

Grant snorted. "Right. Luckily, Max seems to have a lot of people willing to help him." He paused for a second, then said, "He didn't like that you set yourself apart from us."

She shrugged. "I don't want him to miss me when I'm gone."

Grant inclined his head. "You only miss friends if they never come around again."

She shifted on the wooden boards to face him. "Are you offering me the chance to vacation here?

Because I've got to warn you, I will take you up on it. Once I dump the ranch, I'm going to need a break."

He laughed, then surprised her by putting his arm around her shoulders, shifting her so they sat side by side. "You know, one of the best things about having money is being able to find goofy little holes in people's lives and fill them."

Having his arm around her felt so right, so normal, and she was so tired that she had to fight the longing to lean against him and absorb some of his strength.

"By providing vacations?"

"Yeah. Weekends. Plane tickets. Fruit baskets."

She laughed. "Fruit baskets?"

"Not everything's about getting away."

A little too comfortable being this close to him she shifted the conversation to get them back to the real purpose of her being on his island. His autobiography. "Tell me you did that before your accident, and we will have a totally different book on our hands."

"Before my accident I didn't see anything but work."

"Getting hurt changed you?"

The look that came to his dark eyes told her that he realized she was interviewing him again, looking at angles, hoping for secrets.

"Do you ever take a break?"

She wanted to. Right now, with the remnants

of the grief of her own loss mixing with Max's loss, her entire body ached. Life seemed like a long, endless, lonely road.

But she couldn't tell him that. She couldn't confide. She was an employee.

"I've got five weeks left to turn in a manuscript that's as close to publishable as I can make it. I don't have time to—"

He stopped her with a kiss. The kiss he'd almost given her twice.

Her heart stumbled. Her breathing stuttered. Everything inside her woke up and glittered with happiness. She told herself this wasn't right, that she shouldn't get involved with him, then she let herself fall into the kiss. She hadn't kissed anyone in four long years, and it was delicious—he was delicious. Soft, yet demanding.

She reached up to catch his shoulders to steady herself and the feeling of touching him sent delight shimmying through her. She liked this guy that everybody else thought was a holy terror. He'd barely shown her his holy terror side. She'd seen more of his nice guy side. She'd seen someone trying to tell his story. Someone good to a child he hadn't even known he'd had.

And he liked her.

He liked her enough to finally kiss her.

He pulled back. She blinked at him, his strong-featured face, his dark, sensual eyes. She should feel odd, uncomfortable or at least have the sense that kissing had been wrong. But nothing had ever felt as right.

"I've been wanting to do that all day. You seemed so alone."

Disappointment stopped her heart. "You kissed me because you felt sorry for me?"

He snorted. "No. I kissed you because I want you and I usually get what I want. But I need you for the book. Plus, we have a little boy to consider. No skinny-dipping. No inadvertent remarks."

She laughed. Joy tumbled around in her chest, confusing her. She might like and understand him, but she wasn't supposed to even *want* to get romantically involved with him. If that wasn't rule number one between bosses and employees, it should be. She sobered her expression. He was right. He needed her for his book and they did have a little boy to consider.

"Plus, I think anything between us has to be *your* choice." He sniffed a laugh. "Actually, I think you're going to have to seduce me. I'll take that as your proof that us sleeping together won't hurt the book or our relationships with Max."

His presumptuousness made her sputter. "Who says I want you?"

"After the way you kissed me back?" He laughed again. "Nice try. Something's been bubbling between us since you stepped onto my dock. It's starting to annoy me that you're so good at ignoring it when I'm not."

She laughed, but even as her heart told her to open up, to enjoy this, part of her wanted to run. She'd lost her parents. She'd lost a fiancé through a bad choice. She might not be strong enough to handle another loss. Plus, he was nothing like the one guy she'd loved enough to want to marry.

Still, temptation rose and swelled. There really was something between them. He'd made himself vulnerable with his admissions. If nothing else, she had to be honest.

She scooted a few inches away from him. "I'm not as good at ignoring it as you think."

He grinned. "Oh, yeah?"

"Yeah." The rapport between them amazed her, comforted her and scared her silly. How did someone become so close to a person in so little time, with almost no effort? Especially when they really had nothing in common. And with the exception of the things he'd been telling her for his autobiography, they really didn't know each other—

She scooted a little farther away.

He motioned to the distance she'd managed to put between them. "You're saying one thing but doing another. I'm also as concerned as Max was that you won't interact with us."

"I'm an employee."

"So? We like you."

"All right. The truth? I worry about Max getting attached to another person he might lose, and I don't want to get too attached either."

"To me or Max?"

"Either." She shook her head. "Both." She nudged him with her shoulder. "I feel like I'm finally coming out of four years of grief, and I can't go through that again when I lose you when I leave." She nudged him again. "You're very likable."

He laughed. "I have a hundred former employees who will dispute that."

"You have former employees who would probably gape in awe watching you with Max." She caught his gaze. "You're different. Not the same guy who got hit by that car."

"No. I *am* the same guy. We're just in different circumstances. Max needs understanding. I need time to get to know him. And you act like a person who is lost and tired. Is it so wrong that the three of us spend the next five weeks trying to adjust to our new realities?"

"When you put it like that, it seems like the right thing to do."

He shook his head and laughed. "How have you survived the past four years?"

"I have no idea. I woke up one day the owner of a failing ranch. Trying to make that turkey work took every waking minute of every day. I didn't have time to analyze it or myself."

"You found time for ghostwriting."

"That was about ten or twelve weeks out of every year. The rest of the time I was a woman drowning."

"Well, that ends now. Tomorrow, you come out on the boat with us. You might not eat all three meals, but the two you do eat will be with us." His expression became serious. "You need this. You're so sad even Max noticed. Let's all enjoy these next few weeks."

Lola nodded, as her head and her heart battled. She really did need some relaxation, some fun, some interaction with good people while her thoughts sorted themselves.

But, oh, how dangerous that was. She could still feel his kiss on her lips, causing the longing for more to hum through her. But what was more? Laughter and kissing…or a real connection that would find its way into her heart and fill it—

Then break it when it was time for her to leave.

Why couldn't she be the kind of woman who could enjoy herself, have a fling, spend time with a little boy who needed her, then go home with good memories.

Why couldn't she put her vulnerability on hold and simply enjoy herself with no regrets?

CHAPTER SEVEN

GRANT WOKE THE next morning feeling better than he had in years. For the second time in his life, he wasn't a hundred percent sure what he was doing, but buying this island for his recovery had worked out just fine. It had been the best decision of his life.

Which would make propositioning Lola the second-best, if only because he'd learned a thing or two in the past four years about taking time-outs.

His first time-out had been necessary—maybe even forced upon him—because he'd needed to recuperate after his accident. As he'd regained his strength, living on an island had become fun, invigorating. Not fighting with his board or working every waking minute had become a chance to enjoy his wealth and his friends. It had shown him the good side of life, shown him that work had to be rewarded with rest.

He was fairly certain that was what Lola needed right now and if romance came into the picture, so much the better. Not just for him. For her. She needed a space of time when she had no worries, where she didn't ponder her future, when reality was thousands of miles away.

Because reality for him and her and even Max was that they would all be starting over. When they left this island, they'd have to establish new lives and learn how to live them.

All three of them needed this space of time before the real world bombarded them again.

Which was what made his relationship with Lola different than his relationship with his ex. There was an end date. There'd be no marriage, no living together, no arguments. Just fun.

He jogged up the stairs to the third-floor bedrooms and he smiled when he walked past Lola's suite. It might take her awhile to get the courage to seduce him, but they had plenty of time. Despite some rumors about him, he was a patient man when he needed to be.

Plus, he hadn't said he wouldn't entice her in the weeks she took to make up her mind. He had all kinds of fun things in store for her.

He reached Max's room and quietly opened the door just in case Max was sleeping. He wasn't. His son stood on the wraparound deck, looking at the water. He held the sailboat Grant had found online and had delivered to the island, along with a beach ball, a corn hole game, a few Frisbees, a bucket ball game and some extra floaties for the pool.

Closing the door, he stepped inside the bedroom. "Hey, Max!"

Max turned. "Hey, Dad."

Grant didn't think he'd ever get over the emotion that washed through him every time Max called him dad. Part thrill, part warmth, it tightened his chest and softened places in him he didn't realize he had.

"Ready for breakfast?"

"Is Lola awake?"

"Not sure. But it's not appropriate for two gentlemen to knock on her bedroom door."

Max's head tilted.

"We want to give her privacy. She could still be sleeping, or she could be going over her work notes."

Max nodded and they went inside to change him out of his pajamas and into shorts and a T-shirt, then they went downstairs to the dining room.

Denise entered with a smile. "I was thinking you guys might like French toast this morning."

Max's eyes lit. "With cinnamon?"

"Always."

Grant laughed and his thoughts when he woke whispered through him again. This really was a special space of time for him, Max and Lola. Now, he simply had to convince Lola it was okay to take advantage of it.

"French toast it is."

As if she'd timed it, Lola arrived just as Denise entered with two plates of French toast.

"If you want French toast," Denise said, "I can bring you a plate."

Grant said, "She can have mine. I'll wait."

"No waiting," Denise said. "There's more already made."

She left the dining room and Grant caught Lola's gaze. "Good morning."

Her cheeks pinkened as she averted her eyes. "Good morning."

Busy with the syrup, Max said, "Yeah. Good morning."

"Caroline's going to be taking the boys to the mainland this morning. First, they'll see a few tourist attractions, then they're going to the public beach. Caroline says it's good to be with other people sometimes. They'll also have lunch before they return."

Lola smiled at Max. "That sounds amazing."

In his simple, honest way, Max said, "I know."

"Which leaves us almost six hours to work," Grant said, as Denise set his plate of French toast in front of him.

Lola caught his gaze. Uncertainty filled her pretty blue eyes. "I'm not sure how you want to divide up the time."

She was clearly confused about how their lives would change now that he'd suggested they have some fun in the weeks they had together on the island. He would say he was about to teach her that their work and play could be accommodated in special times like the one they were in now, but he didn't want to insult her. Instead, without spelling it out, he set their schedule.

"We have a lot of work to do. You more than me. So, let's factor in time for you to process everything I've said and type up your notes."

"I can type up notes at night," she said, slathering syrup onto her breakfast. "If you want to talk the whole time Max is gone, I'm all for it."

He smiled at her, and she immediately averted her gaze.

Averting her gaze when she'd arrived in the dining room had been natural. But a second time of her not wanting to look in his eyes? That wasn't her. She was smarter, bolder, than this.

Maybe he'd misjudged her? Maybe she wasn't ready for something to happen between them?

Caroline arrived and herded laughing Max and Jeremy into the cruiser to go to the mainland. As Grant stepped away from the boat, Lola stood on the dock behind him, waving to the happy trio.

The boat edged away from the wooden platform then took off toward the tourist town.

Grant inhaled a quick breath. "We are so lucky to have Caroline."

"I know." She hadn't been pleased that Grant

seemed to have arranged for them to be alone the morning after he'd all but told her he wanted to sleep with her. Not just because it was heavy handed, but because they had work to do. Seeing this as her big chance to make sure Grant didn't have any ideas, Lola added, "We need all the work time we can scrape together to get your biography written."

He faced her. Their gazes caught. She wasn't even sure they should have a romance and his tactic of getting everybody out of the house to give them privacy wouldn't push her into doing something she wasn't ready for.

Instead of making a pass or even a suggestion, he turned toward the house and motioned for her to walk with him.

"Absolutely. I've been thinking about my life... you know, things I want to get into the book and I think today might be the day I talk in detail about my work."

She peeked over at him. In a T-shirt and shorts, he looked more like a beach bum than a genius, but he was a genius. He liked his work and wanted to talk about it. In fact, he seemed eager to talk about it.

Maybe arranging for them to be alone wasn't a setup?

Relief tiptoed through her but was quickly replaced by unexpected disappointment. He was good-looking, smart, strong. Why wouldn't she want to make the most of their time together? Why did everything always have to be so serious with her?

Her life was a mess. She would be returning to Montana to face reality. He was offering her almost five weeks of not dwelling on that. Why couldn't she just let go?

Because she was afraid of a broken heart.

Which was ridiculous. If she went into this knowing it was temporary, that she was only looking for a respite, not forever, she should be able to control her emotions. Plus, she also couldn't be angry with him or herself when his autobiography was done, and she got on his cruiser and headed home. She'd been strong before her parents' deaths. And if she really was coming back to herself, she could be strong again.

She took a breath. With the sun already hot, golden rays shimmered around him. Almost as if Fate were saying, "Who cares about reality? Here he is. Yours for a moment. You know better than anyone that there is no such thing as permanent or forever. You should enjoy."

She should!

Still, she couldn't pull the trigger. Even with them alone for hours she couldn't turn to him and kiss him senseless. She needed another day or two to either assure herself she could handle this or get herself to the point where she could absolutely say no to his suggestion. Say no to kisses that felt so right. Say no to having someone she could talk to, open up with. Say no to moonlight walks on the beach, swimming, waking up with him in paradise—

Obviously oblivious to her thoughts, Grant kept talking. "I don't think people have any idea of how hard I worked. Everybody assumes that being a genius smooths your path…and in a way, it does. I see things others don't. But that doesn't mean I don't spend long hours sorting through ideas, combining ideas, figuring out how to turn ideas into products that have value. And don't even get me started on marketing."

Excitement skittered along her nerve endings. She might not be able to decide about a romance between them, but this morning she would hear what it was like to be a genius. This was the part of reporting she loved. Getting the inside story.

"Actually, that reminds me of something I've been wanting to ask. I'm telling you my life in segments. You're not just typing out what I told you. You're piecing it all together."

"Sort of." Glad he was ready to work, and give her time to think about the romance end of things, she led the way to the house. "There are two ways to tell your story. I can do it in segments like work, education, creating and leading. Or I can put it together chronologically, taking those segments you've been dictating and weaving them into a timeline. My instincts are telling me the timeline is the way to go. But I haven't made up my mind yet."

He nodded.

They spent the next two hours in the office with him talking about work. Lola was very glad for her recorder because she would be researching the technical terms he tossed around as if everyone knew them. Like most people, she had a grasp of the basics about computers, software and the way the world had changed with a few simple inventions. But Grant was a computer guy. She wouldn't sell him short by simplifying concepts that should be complex to demonstrate that he deserved the success he'd found.

They stopped for lunch, which she refused. Her brain popped with too many ideas to sit and eat a sandwich and talk about nothing. She returned to her room to search the technical things he'd spoken of so casually.

Working on the deck, she heard the cruiser return and glanced at her watch. It was after two o'clock. Grant had left her alone to work.

Watching as happy Caroline led her two boys into the house like a short string of baby chicks, she wondered about all those employees who'd complained about Grant.

Oh, she knew he probably was a taskmaster of a sort, but he seemed particularly attuned to her need for time to work on her own. Surely, he'd also realized employees needed time to implement the ideas he had in his head. What could have happened to make him lose his temper and fire so many people?

She carefully approached the subject after dinner. They'd eaten in the dining room. Max and Benjamin Franklin had had a little beach time. Then Grant had taken his little boy upstairs to get into pajamas. Now, they were alone, on the pool patio, surrounded by the sounds of the ocean and a million stars.

"Of course, I gave people time to work on projects."

"Were you the kind of boss who interrupted work sessions? Did you watch over their shoulders?"

He laughed. "Next you'll be asking if I used a whip to prod them or put a ball and chain on their ankles to make sure they couldn't leave their desks."

"So your Laningham the Destroyer name is all about that month you kept firing people?"

"That and the fact that I'm a perfectionist." He caught her gaze. "Most people aren't, you know? To them, good enough is good enough. But it can't be when you're coming up with new products." He shoved his chair away from the umbrella table. "Beer?"

As always, the patio was saved from darkness by the lights of the pool. The heat of the night air was alleviated by a soft breeze. A full, bright moon hung over the ocean.

His explanation satisfied part of her curiosity about the month before he was ousted, but not all of it. There was something missing. Maybe even something he didn't fully understand himself?

Still, she had the sense this wasn't the time to push. And even if it wasn't the night to seduce him, either, the quiet, the moon and the breeze lured her to relax.

"How about a cocktail? What do you have behind that bar?"

"What do you want?"

"I love margaritas and Cosmos…can you make either of those?"

"The margaritas are premixed. I never found a recipe for one that guests liked better than what I could buy already made. The Cosmo I'm pretty good at making."

"I'll take a margarita." She ambled up to the bar and slid onto a stool. "I have to ask. Did you learn to bartend for a reason?"

"You mean like did I bartend while I was at university?"

"Yeah."

"No. My parents paid for my education and before you say anything I knew I was lucky. I've thanked them for that."

"But?"

"No buts. I was lucky. I thanked them because it was the right thing to do."

She thought about that as he poured ice and

the premixed margarita into a blender. He hit the button. The noise disturbed the perfect peace of the island for a solid minute, while he retrieved a glass and rubbed the rim in salt. When the blender stopped, he poured the frozen margarita into the glass and handed it to her.

"You are so good at that."

"I think I'm a natural." He sucked in air as he looked around the patio. "When I was recovering, there wasn't much I could do. But I noticed a hole of a sort when my friends would come down to check on me. Everybody could grab a beer but not everybody could make a cocktail. So, while they were back at work doing their day jobs, I learned to mix drinks. Got Caroline drunk twice. Denise was a better taste tester."

Lola laughed. "Who would have thought."

"Those two were as important to me and my recovery as my physical therapists and doctors. We've become close over the years. I'll never sell this place. It'll be a weekend getaway for me."

"And your two best friends."

"And my two best friends."

He grabbed a beer for himself and took a seat on the stool beside hers. "Okay, enough about me. My head's about to explode from this morning's session and you spent most of the afternoon transcribing. You've got to be tired too."

"I am."

He nudged his head in the direction of the chaise

lounges. "So maybe we just sit and watch the ocean for a few minutes. No talking. Just sipping our drinks."

"Sounds good to me."

She noticed again that he wasn't pushing her toward the relationship he was so sure they both wanted. She stretched out on the chaise, letting the sound of the surf hypnotize her.

"I was so bored during therapy."

She laughed and poked him playfully. "I thought you said no talking."

He faced her. "This isn't me talking for the biography. This is me talking to a friend."

"Okay."

"You see people in wheelchairs, and you recognize they're injured but subconsciously you're thinking they can still get around so it's not that big of a deal." He glanced out over the ocean. "But people have no idea what someone in a wheelchair gives up. What they are missing. Especially freedom."

"Sounds like your injury gave you a lot of life lessons."

"And perspective and a sense of appreciation."

"You talked about your friends coming to your aid and visiting. Did your parents help out?"

"Because they were already retired, living in Key West, they made one visit to the hospital in Manhattan and one trip here once I was stable."

Her face scrunched. "But you were injured, and they're doctors."

"Yes, and they got access to my charts and talked to my specialists and told me I was fine."

"If you were in a wheelchair, you weren't fine."

"After looking at my charts, they knew I would heal." He snorted. "Actually, that's how I took it. When my parents told me I was fine, I realized they were essentially telling me that there was nothing so broken it couldn't heal. I reasoned that meant I had to do my physical therapy and then I'd be fine."

"They didn't visit you?"

"They made the initial trip to the hospital to get the scoop on my injuries. They visited me here once. But I preferred that they stay away. Healing is hard. Therapy is hard work. I didn't want them around watching—criticizing."

Her brain went blank. *He didn't want them here.* Maybe he didn't want anybody here? Except a house manager and a cook.

And his friends, whom she would love to meet.

But that explained why he and Caroline were so close. Denise, too.

The breeze billowed around them in the darkness. She thought about who Grant had been and who he'd become, and amazement filled her. Maybe while she listened to and eventually wrote his story, she should be taking a page from his book. Learning from him. He knew how to accept things, to take things in stride. He also knew how to live in the moment, do the next logical thing, and enjoy what he had.

That's what was missing in her life. The lesson she should have learned in the last four years. Hiding hadn't helped. Losing herself in work hadn't helped.

Accepting her losses, accepting that she'd made a mistake and would have to sell her ranch, accepting that she had to rebuild her life, those had helped.

Grant had helped. Hearing his story had helped.

She finished her margarita and took the glass to the bar. "I guess I should be getting inside."

He rose from the chaise. "Me too. Tomorrow is another fishing day for Max and Jeremy."

She remembered that he'd said he wanted her to go with them the next time they went out on the boat. Temptation rose and she couldn't quite quash it. She was tired of being alone. Tired of hoping for things that wouldn't happen. Ready to accept reality and move on.

And maybe that's the realization Grant had found after his accident when he learned how to accept his life—enjoy reality instead of wishing for what couldn't be.

Enjoy reality instead of wishing for what couldn't be.

That was what she needed to do.

She felt as if someone had opened the windows

of her life and let fresh air inside. Felt as if she could breathe. Felt for the first time in years that everything was going to be okay.

They walked into the downstairs family room. She turned to the left to go to the stairway, but he turned right and picked up a remote.

"Twenty minutes of a ball game wouldn't hurt."

She laughed and walked over to him again. She smiled up at him, then pressed her hands to his cheeks. "You're checking up on your team."

He winced. "Maybe a little."

"You're so interesting."

He chuckled. "If another person had said that I'd probably be insulted. Coming from you though, I know that's a compliment."

"It is a compliment."

Unable to resist, she rose to her tiptoes and pressed her mouth to his quickly, completely. But he didn't let her pull away. He caught her elbows and kept her where she was, deepening the kiss, opening a part of her that had been closed for four long years. She felt the strength of him, the surety. If there would ever be a person she could trust with her life, herself, even for only a few weeks, it would be him.

The certainty of that scared her as much as it comforted her. How could a person not fall in love with him?

That was really the problem. There was no

question that she'd enjoy being with him, but could she give him up?

She'd given up her fiancé and hadn't cared as long as she was busy traveling. But when her life stopped when her parents died, she'd realized what she'd thrown away. Selling her ranch would keep her busy for a while…but as soon as it was sold and she was on her own again, would she miss Grant? Or would she regret not taking advantage of their time together?

She pulled away and he smiled at her. The urge to let go and let nature take its course with them tiptoed through her.

Then she remembered she had always been the smart one, the reasonable one. The only time she'd let go and done something without thinking it through—buy a ranch—she'd made a huge mistake.

Even if it meant she'd miss out on something wonderful, she could not afford another huge mistake in her life.

She would take the time to think this through. But the odds had gone up significantly in his favor.

CHAPTER EIGHT

LOLA STEPPED AWAY, studying his face for a few more seconds, thinking thoughts he was absolutely positive he'd never be privy to. For a woman who made her living poking into other people's lives she held her own story close to the vest. She'd told him bits and pieces, snippets of her past that showed she understood the things he'd told her, but she never gave away enough that he felt he knew the real her—the complete her.

He probably never would.

She turned to go to the stairway. "Good night."

"Good night."

Shaking his head, he picked up the remote and found the Lions game. Everything inside him pulsed with life but she'd been able to walk away.

Still, she was the one who'd initiated that kiss.

The hot, prickly feeling of success surged through him. He told himself he'd made progress that night, and to a degree he had, but in the grand scheme of things he really hadn't. Losing her parents, then making such a big life change—

one that had blown up in her face—hadn't scared her as much as it had scarred her.

Oddly, that was probably why he related to her. He understood her enough that he would never push. He might try enticing her, but he'd never push her. He'd lose all the possible fun they could have together, the friendship they could probably forge, before he'd push her.

He plopped to the sofa. Two strikes and a runner on third should have held his attention, instead it kept straying to Lola. He closed his eyes remembering her softness and her strength. He had the weirdest feeling she didn't know how strong she was but if she ever picked up on that she would be unstoppable.

And tremendously fun to fool around with.

The thought made him groan and though he tried to focus on the baseball game, he couldn't. He went to the primary suite equal parts turned on and exhausted. The thought of the busy morning he'd have with the boys forced him to his bed. The time spent in the pool with them had left him depleted enough that he fell asleep immediately. Unfortunately, morning came in what felt like twenty minutes.

He crawled out of bed, just a little bit sore. Wounds from his accident sometimes rebelled, but a hot shower and some topical ointment for pain were usually enough to get him moving. Once he started moving, he simply kept moving until his body was awake and responding normally.

He and Max ate breakfast alone. He waited for Lola with the nervousness of a guy debating asking the pretty girl in high school for a date. But she never came to the dining room.

Assuming she was already working in her suite, he fought back the disappointment, then did his fatherly duties of rounding up his crew and preparing to take them fishing. When everything was on the boat, he, Max and Jeremy marched across the dock. They jumped in the boat, ready to head out.

Two seconds before he would have shoved off, Lola came running down the weather-beaten boards.

A hand on her big sunhat, she called, "Wait for me!"

Grant helped her into the boat. A little clumsy in her flip-flops and unaccustomed to getting into a cruiser, she all but fell into his arms.

The moment caught and held. It felt so normal, so natural for her to be in his arms that he simply enjoyed her. Her crazy need for independence. The way she could get him to talk without even trying. The yearning he saw in her eyes every time he caught her off guard.

She studied his face. He couldn't tell what she was looking for and didn't know if she found it when she inched away from him, but it was one of the happiest moments of his life. He almost couldn't believe that she'd joined them—and that she hadn't pulled away when she'd fallen into his arms. He didn't feel ice chips melting away, he felt life returning to her spirit.

He grinned at her. "Nice hat."

"My mother always told me to be prepared." She took a breath, smiled at Max. "You said this would be awesome."

He gaped at her as if he couldn't believe she'd doubted him. "It is!"

Time stopped for Grant again. All his money couldn't buy the emotions that swam through him at seeing Max happy, and Lola in the boat, willing to have some fun.

The air filled with promise, and he faced his crew. "Well, let's get going then."

As he eased the boat away from the dock, Jeremy and Max—both in swimming trunks and life vests—knelt on the bench seat to watch the wake and feel the spray on their little boy faces.

Lola slipped out of the sweater she had over her tank top and shorts. Grant snickered and shook his head. Her mother must have been something for her to hold onto her advice to always be prepared as if it was the only thing she had left of her—

He frowned. Maybe it was? Memories, advice—that was it. That was all she had of her parents. He supposed if his parents had given him loving advice instead of lectures, he might want to remember it too.

But they hadn't. They hadn't been around for most of his life, and when the result of that was a tragedy, they felt they should be able to waltz in and pretend nothing had happened.

Well, he wouldn't let them.

He stopped the boat at one of his favorite fishing spots. The boys raced for the rod and bait, eager today because they knew what they were doing. The sun was hot. The kids were happy. Lola also had her face raised to enjoy the warmth that surrounded them.

He wouldn't let negative thoughts ruin this good day.

That was how *he* survived.

Lola savored the warm rays on her face, but she knew she couldn't stay that way long or she'd sunburn. She found the sunscreen Caroline always packed for the boys as Grant talked them through the process of baiting the hook and casting off. It surprised her that the boys themselves weren't fishing, but they seemed perfectly happy to kneel on the bench seat and watch Grant do all the work.

She studied the rod and noted its size, remembering from a fishing trip or two with her dad that grouper could be large—probably difficult to reel in. Which was undoubtedly why Grant was doing all the heavy lifting.

"Why not try for something smaller so the boys can fish too?"

Max and Jeremy gaped at her as if she'd said something sacrilegious.

Grant laughed. "We like to eat grouper."

"Yeah. We like grouper," Max and Jeremy echoed.

Grant had once said that Max reminded him of himself when he was younger and this morning, she saw it. Not just the physical similarities of bone structure that showed Max would someday be tall like Grant. But the idiosyncrasies. The way they held their heads or looked out over the water. Even the way they walked.

The boys returned their attention to the water. With the rod anchored on some kind of holder, Grant watched the sway of the line. Lola got more comfortable on the seat, suddenly wishing she had a book. Not because she was bored but because it seemed to be a good place to read. While her three companions had fun, watching the line, hoping for a fish, she could be reading in the warmth of the sun with the ocean sparkling around them.

Eventually, they caught a fish. Max and Jeremy danced as Grant displayed some serious fishing skills, reeling in the big fish: the grouper they wanted.

"This is dinner," Grant said proudly. "Jeremy, do you want to stay and eat with us?"

He nodded eagerly.

Lola shook her head, wishing she could write about this. No matter what Grant said about the perfectionist he was when he worked, *this* was the real Grant Laningham. And this was the real story. Recovery and change. So much so that even a surprise like a child arriving unexpectedly hadn't fazed him.

They drove back to the dock. Max and Jeremy raced ahead to tell Caroline about the big fish.

Lola waited for Grant. She followed him to an unexpected room on the first level of his house where he prepped the fish for cooking.

She glanced around at the gray, cement block room with an unremarkable table, a ladder, some tools. "This does not match the rest of the house."

"Actually, this is the most practical room of the house."

"I suppose." She faced him. "The boys really enjoyed the trip."

"I did too." He laughed. "I'm fishing alone when there aren't any guests. I love having built-in companions."

"You also seem to like teaching them. Have you ever thought of teaching as your second act?"

He gaped at her. "You're kidding, right?"

"Imagine what you could impart to students at the university level."

He shook his head. "No. And don't suggest I do a TED Talk either."

She laughed heartily. "Are we going to work today?"

"This afternoon." He glanced at her. "Caroline will keep the kids. I thought we'd invite her to dinner too, since Jeremy wants to eat dinner here."

"Sounds fun."

"Okay. I'll meet you in the office at about two." He paused. "Unless you want to join us for lunch? I'm grilling hot dogs. There might even be potato chips."

"With all this sumptuous-looking fish for dinner? I'm saving my appetite."

She left him tending to his fish and headed to her suite where she opened her laptop. She knew Grant didn't want Max in his story, but something inside her had to write up what she'd watched that morning. Not the events, but the emotions. Max loving his dad. Grant teaching, nurturing those two little boys. Giving them not just his time but an experience they might carry with them forever.

With all that out of her system, she consulted her outline, fleshed it out a bit, took transcribed notes and began arranging them into chunks of the book.

The oddest thing happened. As she arranged, wrote and rewrote passages of his conversations, she heard Grant's voice in her head as if he were reciting the words as she typed.

She heard his voice.

She smiled. When she heard the voice of her subject, she knew the story had found its footing. She really was telling *his* story.

She felt so good about the biography that after their session that afternoon, she again showered and dressed for dinner. She tightened her long tresses into a bun at the top of her head with tendrils of curls falling haphazardly around her face and neck.

When she stepped onto the patio, the boys were in the pool with Benjamin Franklin and Caroline lounged on a chaise, enjoying a cocktail.

"You're not going to get her drunk," she chastised Grant.

Caroline snorted. "I survived the learning-to-bartend years. I now know my limit. I also know when to stay away from him because he's in the mood to entertain."

Lola laughed.

"But he's especially happy with me tonight because my family's going to Busch Gardens for the weekend, and I asked to take Max."

"Oh?" She glanced at Grant who was peering at the fish.

"Honestly, my sisters all have granddaughters. There's never been a little boy for Jeremy to run with. So, Max would be a welcome addition."

"Sounds fun."

"It will be," Grant agreed. "The kid needs all the

breaks and fun he can get right now. An amusement park with a bunch of kids fits the bill." He pointed at the closed grill. "Grouper's just about ready." His head tilted. For the first time since she arrived, he really looked at her. "You dressed up again. You must be pleased with what you wrote today."

It had stopped unnerving her that he didn't merely see everything, he had a way of analyzing what he saw and keeping it in that steel trap mind of his. Instead, she accepted it. That was part of who he was, and that part was interesting and sometimes even amazing.

She strolled to the chaise beside Caroline. "Yes. I am extremely pleased. Not just with the work we did today but with the project. It finally seems like it's coming together."

"When do I get to read it?"

She frowned, pretending she wasn't sure that was a good idea, though she liked having her subjects read the story as it was evolving. But it was always better if Grant believed something was his idea. He wasn't the only one who noticed things. Noticing things was her job. She never argued with her subconscious that saw as much as his did.

"If you promise to keep in mind that this is little more than an outline that's being fleshed out, I could let you read it any time you want."

He perked up. "Really?"

"It's your story. Plus, reading at this stage might remind you of things you want to add. Points you want to make."

"I feel like I'm already hitting all the highlights."

"You'll be surprised by how much reading a draft will jog your memories."

He smiled and nodded. "Okay. Shoot me an attachment in an email."

"Okay."

"Want a drink?"

She shook her head. "It's such a hot day, I think I need water."

He rounded the bar. "Water it is." He tossed a bottle to her.

She caught it like an expert.

"You played ball."

She shrugged. "Everybody plays softball at some point in their life."

"Were you good?" Caroline asked.

"Good enough that I got a scholarship to a small university. Once I got my first two years in and knew what I wanted my major to be, I shifted to a bigger school. One with a respected journalism program."

"I saw you on TV," Caroline said. "I didn't recognize you when you first arrived because I hadn't put two and two together yet, but once Grant told me you'd been a foreign correspondent, bingo, I remembered you."

"That was a really fun time in my life."

Grant snorted. "Getting shot at was fun?"

"Meeting people from all over the world was fun. Seeing cultures. I would come home from an assignment and my parents would put on a pot of coffee and quiz me." The memory of it surprised her, not with its clarity but with the jolt of happiness that accompanied it.

Caroline laughed. "I'd probably have a million questions too."

Grant peeked at the fish, then yelled to the boys. "Dinner's almost ready. Grab some dry towels."

The boys jumped out of the pool without question. Grant brought the fish to the table, along with containers of steamed vegetables that he'd cooked on the grill too. Jeremy sat by Caroline at the table. Max sat beside Grant. Because the table was round, when Lola sat beside Max she was also beside Jeremy.

The patio filled with the sounds of everyone passing dishes of food, filling plates and taking that first bite.

The air stilled. Everyone savored. Then a communal groan rose around them.

"This is fabulous!" Lola said. "My compliments to the chef."

"I researched cooking grouper a few years ago."

Of course, he had.

"This technique is the one everyone seems to like. Now it's my go-to way to prepare it."

"Well, whatever you did, this fish is amazing."

Caroline brought up the subject of Lola's travels again and did ask a good bit of the questions she'd said she would have. The boys gobbled their food, hardly interested in Lola's life and went inside to play a video game.

The adults stayed at the table, talking the way she and her parents had when she would arrive home from an assignment.

As Caroline nodded in response to something Grant said, and Grant rose to clean the grill, a weird sense fell over Lola. She was talking about her parents without missing them… No. She was talking with other people the way she always had with her parents and not missing them.

She was making a friend of Caroline. A handsome, sexy, extremely successful man was interested in her. She'd been swimming with Max. She'd gone on a boat. And had fun.

The feeling intensified until Lola recognized it.

She wasn't moving on with her life—a term people said when they spoke of her parents, a term she hated. The jumble of feelings she'd had since her parents' deaths had settled enough that the person she'd been was finally able to see and talk and come out again.

Grant's voice intruded on her revelation. "I'm going to save this for lunch tomorrow," he said, reaching for the platter with the leftover fish.

"The boys could eat hot dogs every day," Caroline said. "But it wouldn't hurt to toss something different in their menus."

Grant laughed. "I agree."

Lola's head tilted as she watched him. He was so different, so much more likable than he'd been portrayed before his accident. And he liked her. She also liked him. No, she was enthralled by him. The person she'd been before her parents' passing would have seduced him the night he'd told her he wanted to sleep with her.

That realization intensified, bringing some conclusions. If the fog of grief and the burden of the trouble she'd made for herself when she bought the ranch really were lifting, she would be enjoying the hell out of the rest of the time she had here. Time with Grant. Time with Max. Time on an island where no one would criticize or question her. Where she could experiment with the idea that she was coming back to life and see if it was as real as it felt.

And maybe that's exactly what she should do.

CHAPTER NINE

As GOOD AS her word, Lola had sent Grant the draft of his autobiography. Because it was mostly an outline and notes with a few fleshed-out passages, he'd read through it before he'd fallen asleep that night.

When they met in his office the next morning, he was ready with comments.

"At this point, it seems like you're highlighting my logic. It reads funny to me."

"It reads funny to you because you're the guy we're writing about." Dressed in her usual shorts and T-shirt, with her hair down, she leaned across the desk, as if trying to see what page or excerpt had made him feel odd. "That's one of the reasons I like my clients to see every stage of the book. The next time you read what we have you will be accustomed to reading about yourself."

"It's first person. My voice. I know I'm reading about myself."

"See…that right there. Knowing it's your voice is what we are aiming for."

He frowned at her. She grinned at him. Her pretty blue eyes were lit with excitement. Even her pert little nose looked cute this morning.

"So, we're on the right track?"

"We are," she assured him in her confident, happy tone. "But if you want to discuss the logic thread, I'm using that to demonstrate that you weren't a bad person or even a taskmaster—"

His eyebrows rose.

"You're driven by common sense and logic."

He understood what she was saying. He simply wasn't sure he liked it. "You make me sound like an android."

"In the first draft maybe. But as we flesh out the story, we'll flesh out your character."

"Now it sounds like we're making things up."

She laughed gaily. "No. We'll be adding layers to your personality so that the logic thread will recede into the background of the story. It will still be there, guiding readers, but it will be more subtle. And they will be accustomed to the way you worked when we get to the point where we have to talk about the month you got rid of an employee every day…the month that led to you being fired."

He said nothing. She might have avoided mentioning this before now because she'd latched on to a reasonable explanation for his behavior and was setting that up. But a shimmer of a memory rose in him. His sister. Her suicide. Gio working his magic to keep the story out of the press.

He tried to fight the memory because, like Max, he didn't want his sister in his autobiography. Her death might serve to explain things, but it felt wrong. Like an excuse for bad behavior. He didn't make excuses. He took responsibility.

Plus, Lola was better at making his actions sound reasonable than she knew. She was portraying him as human, as a person who made mistakes but moved on. When the time came to talk about the reason his board fired him, she would describe him being out of control that month because they were behind schedule. After the buildup to that point, people would see his temper as the natural result of a perfectionist not being able to get his work done.

He knew that's how she would handle it. Because he knew that's how she saw it. She was extremely good at what she did, not just a pretty face on the news. Though her face was extremely pretty, especially when she was happy.

When he realized pondering his life and the book had stopped, and he was just sitting in his chair, staring at her, liking the way her hair flowed around her and the happy expression on her face, he snapped himself back to real life again.

"What you're saying is that we're on schedule."

"I think so. In another two weeks this draft

won't be a draft. It will be a manuscript and then we'll nitpick."

He laughed at her choice of words. "I am known for that."

"Which is why there's time built in for you to nitpick to your heart's delight."

"Or we could spend that time on the boat."

She laughed. "You got me out once—"

"Max got you out once. I haven't made any headway in getting you to relax."

She leaned back in her chair. "Sure, you have. I've had drinks with you. We've also sat on your patio enjoying the breeze."

"And you always questioned me. Interviewed me. I'd like a night when we could just be ourselves."

"Really?"

"You know, with Caroline taking Max for the weekend, we could fly to the Virgin Islands." As the suggestion formed in his mind, he liked it more and more. "We could have fancy private dinners. We could dance in the moonlight…and stay over."

"Stay over?"

"I'd book us separate rooms."

He watched as she considered that. When she didn't reply, he said, "Think it through. This time next month you will be on a ranch in Montana. Probably slogging through wet fields with a real estate agent, hoping he or she has a client on the line who wants it. And you'll be cursing your-self, thinking you should have taken the tropical getaway with me."

She laughed. "Yeah. I haven't forgotten that whole mess is waiting for me."

"So come away with me."

He rose from his seat behind the desk and leaned against it, in front of her. "This time next month, I'll be facing work the likes of which I haven't done in four years. I didn't leave in good standing. The world's moved on without me. It's going to be the challenge of a lifetime…so maybe do it for me?"

Her eyes softened. She really was a nice per-son. Someone who genuinely connected with others. Someone who felt deeply. He couldn't imagine what she'd gone through when she lost her parents. But he knew enough from what hap-pened after he lost his sister to understand why Lola had broken.

"All right. We can use a rest. We'll return with our minds fresh and ready to go back to work."

The shock of her agreeing hit him like a punch in the gut. Still, he pretended to be casual. "Okay. I'll make the arrangements."

He walked behind the desk again. They talked about the book a bit more, first themes, then whether it was best to set out the story in topics or write it on a timeline, a chronological order of events. In the end he decided he liked the timeline. Technically, what he'd already read followed a timeline so why mess with something that was working?

Then she asked about his first company, which led to him admitting his humble beginnings, sleeping on Brad's couch so he could put all his money into his start-up. That segued into talking about the lawsuit that had nearly crushed him until he saw at trial that the testimony about his product was an advertisement that it was a step forward in software development and suddenly sales went through the roof.

"Interesting."

He sighed. "What's interesting now?"

She laughed. "I don't mean interesting as a way to nudge you to explain. It really is interesting that you saw that the trial itself was an advertisement for your software."

"I see everything."

"Yeah. You do."

She stretched, appearing to ease a kink out of her back before she rose, but all he saw was softness, feminine curves.

"I think that's enough for today. Especially if we're going away. I'll need to have all this transcribed and integrated into the document so I can rest while we're gone."

He nodded, still unable to believe she'd agreed to go away with him, but not about to question his luck. He knew he'd probably never get this chance again. As she walked to the door, he called, "Pack for two days."

She stopped. "Two?"

"Caroline said they were going away for the weekend. That's two days."

She sniffed a laugh, shook her head and walked out of the room.

He got on the phone. If he only had two days, he would make the best of them.

Friday morning, Max grinned foolishly as he headed to the door with Caroline and Jeremy.

"We'll be back on Sunday night. Probably late," Caroline said, guiding the two boys who walked ahead of her. "Did you talk to Denise about spending time with Benjamin Franklin?"

Grant said, "She said she'll bring her kids to feed him so he'll get some playtime."

Caroline laughed. "I doubt he needs that. That old, tired dog might be happy to see us go."

Grant snorted.

Lola watched him and Max, looking for signs that time away wasn't a good idea. But Max was excited, and Grant was like a kid before Christmas. Either he needed this break from suddenly becoming a dad and trying to organize the story of his life—

Or he was excited about the *other* things this trip could mean.

Fear tried to steal her breath. In her room, finishing her packing, she reminded herself she wasn't a person prone to fear. She'd traveled the world. And she really had been shot at.

Plus, Grant had said that if anything happened between them, she would have to initiate it.

She had no reason to believe he'd changed his mind. Especially since he'd said he was booking two rooms.

Ten minutes later, she met him in the foyer.

"Ready?"

She smiled at him. "Do you really think a little scruff on your jaw and sunglasses will keep people from recognizing you?"

He hoisted his duffel bag to his shoulder. "You'd be surprised what throws people off. Plus, where we're going is exclusive. There will be people there who don't want to be recognized either. If they recognize me, there'll be like a silent pact that passes between us. Everybody's there for privacy and to relax. Nobody fangirls another guest."

"Well, this should be fun."

He motioned for her to leave the house and head for the dock. Instead of Jason, Grant drove the cruiser, surprising her. He docked in a spot with his name on it then a limo took them to a private airstrip on the mainland. Even on a private jet, the flight to the Virgin Islands was a little longer than Lola expected. Another limo met them and took them to a dock where they boarded another boat that took them to the quiet island filled with trees.

She was just about to mention that she hoped the resort was worth the effort to get there, when they arrived at a white beach with a main building that looked like a big tiki bar and a cluster of smaller tiki huts surrounding it.

Grant pointed at it, as an employee of the resort unloaded their bags. "That's the common area, used mostly for registration. Over there—" he said, pointing to the right "—is a piano bar. Just beyond that is a five-star restaurant."

"Wow." She glanced around. "This certainly beats the accommodations in a war zone."

He laughed. "Yes. It's a different kind of travel than what you're accustomed to."

With a resort employee scurrying to take their bags to their villa, they checked in then walked along a cobblestone path through gardens and wild foliage, toward their private oasis. When they turned left and walked twenty or thirty feet along a path thick with trees and plants, she realized they'd probably been passing well-hidden villas all along.

Grant opened the elaborate leaded glass door and they stepped into a great room. Dark beams in the ceiling contrasted the white walls. Folding doors had been opened to expose their private section of beach where two well-padded chaise lounges awaited them on the white sand that led to the bluest water Lola had ever seen.

"Wow."

"I've been here before. You can mingle or your stay can be totally private, a two-day retreat where we don't have to talk to anyone."

"I thought you said you were getting us two rooms."

"This villa has two bedrooms."

His answer was so casual that she wondered if he even remembered that he'd said he wanted her to seduce him.

She didn't have time to ponder that as he pointed right, outside the folding doors, to a patio with a linen-covered table. "We can eat all three meals there. We can have a chef come here to cook for us. Or we can order off a menu." He smiled. "Like room service."

He gestured beyond the table to a pergola with white linen strips that wove through the beams, which could be drawn for privacy or left as they were to allow sunbathing.

"We can get massages there and even have drinks by the pool." A silver cart covered in white linen didn't quite conceal the refrigerator below the main tray that sat beside a sparkling pool. "I asked for the place to be stocked with beer, wine, water and the makings of margaritas."

She couldn't stop another, "Wow," as she gazed at the absolutely perfect space filled with cool sea air that blew in through the open doors. "So, this is how the other half lives."

"I wouldn't say half." He laughed. "The lucky one percent is who you'll meet here."

She faced him. "If we decide to mingle."

He shrugged. "If we decide to mingle."

"You're seriously not afraid of being recognized?"

He laughed. "I told you. Even people who recognize me won't approach us. Everybody's here for privacy. Everybody respects that."

He plopped on the sofa. "What do you want to do?"

"I think a walk on the beach would be nice."

"Me too. Then we can have lunch and swim. But after that I have something special planned for dinner."

"Really." She'd brought out her flirty voice. Not just because she could see how much trouble he'd gone to to make their two days whatever they wanted them to be; but because they were delaying real life. Living in the moment. She refused to spoil the fantasy for herself or him.

He laughed, rose from the sofa, and slid his arms around her waist. "You're not going to charm the surprise out of me so don't even try."

"I've gotten you to tell me more about yourself and your life than you probably planned. I'll bet I can get you to spill your secret evening."

"You're on. Of course, I should warn you that I

intend to sleep by the pool most of the afternoon, so your badgering time is limited."

She sniffed. "I don't badger."

"You could though," he said, before dropping a quick kiss on her mouth. "You have that in you. Like a determination to get the story could inspire you to push until you made politicians weep."

He headed for the open doors to the beach.

She scrambled after him. "Oh, yeah? So why do you like me then?"

He stopped, faced her. Rather than tease, he got deadly serious. "You keep me on my toes. I like that."

She laughed, then slipped off her shoes before following him out into the sunshine, eager to get *her* toes in the soft white sand.

They walked fifteen minutes out and fifteen minutes back. Enough to feel the tension leave their bodies. Warm from the sun, they spent an hour playing in the pool, then true to his word, he fell asleep on a chaise lounge. A few minutes later she drifted off too. Two hours after that, she awoke, totally awed by the fact that she'd let herself rest.

When she saw the time, she left the pool area and went to the room in which the hotel staff had put her luggage. It all felt weird. She knew he wanted her. Yet he had her things put into a separate room. He held her hand walking along the water. Yet he hadn't made a pass at her.

She thought about it all in the shower, washing her bounty of hair and rinsing off sunblock. He showed her he liked her without being overbearing. And without seducing her. He'd said that was her choice, so she'd have to do the seducing.

She simply wasn't sure how. He was different than anyone she'd ever dated or slept with. For as interested as she was in him, she also recognized he was special. Something inside her didn't want to risk the relationship they had by saying or doing something wrong. And sex changed things. Even between friends. *Especially* between friends.

And then there was their working relationship. How would that change?

Wrapped in the soft white robe provided by the resort, she left the bathroom and headed to her duffel bag. She'd packed her little black dress and actually considered wearing it but decided to save it for the following day when they might eat at the restaurant or visit the piano bar.

She carried it to the closet to hang it, and when she opened the door, three gowns sparkled at her. One was red. One was pale blue. The third was basic black, with subtle sequins that made it sparkle in such a way that it looked like it was moving.

She hung her simple sheath in the closet, then examined the gowns. All three were her size. She considered that this was another service of the resort, then she remembered that Grant Laningham was the most organized problem solver she'd ever met.

And he had a big plan for this evening.

Maybe a plan that required her to wear a gown?

A thrill of happiness danced through her. It was like playing dress-up. And if he hadn't had them sent to her room, and the resort provided them, then maybe she would surprise him by showing up at dinnertime dressed like a princess.

This night was all about fantasy. They'd left reality behind for a few days. She would more than play along. She would do her part.

She carefully did her hair and nails, listening for signs that Grant had come in from his extremely long nap by the pool, but she heard nothing. Considering that her room was at the end of a long corridor she realized she might not hear him enter the great room.

When her hair, nails and makeup were done, she slipped into the red dress. Though it was gorgeous, she wanted to try on the pale blue. That one she loved. Strapless, in a simple style that caressed every curve of her body, the dress was subtly sexy. It was tasteful enough that she could have been going to the opera or even dinner in Manhattan. But the way it flowed over her curves left nothing to the imagination about the shape of her body.

It was naughty but not obvious. Just what she wanted.

Unfortunately, she didn't have shoes to match. Then she laughed. Who cared? If they were staying in their private oasis for the evening, why not be barefoot in a gown?

If they were going out, she could make do with her black pumps. After all, they'd be hidden beneath the flowing skirt.

She left her room and stopped. Hundreds of candles had been placed around the main room.

Careful, she walked down the corridor. When she reached the great room, she saw Grant standing in the center. Dressed in a tux, he held a single red rose.

Her heart stuttered. "This is lovely."

He gave her the rose and held out his hand. "This is just the start." He nodded once and music flowed around them. She noticed a string quartet standing in a corner of the patio.

She put her hand in his and he drew her to him for a quick kiss. The feeling of being Cinderella flitted through her.

"Dinner is on the patio."

She followed him out to the linen-covered table with tall candles and a bottle of champagne chilling in a bucket beside it. As he pulled out her chair, an older gentleman, also in a tux appeared by the side of the table. He set salads at each place.

Grant said, "Thank you."

The waiter said, "The main course is chicken marsala risotto."

She smiled at Grant. "Sounds wonderful."

He leaned across the table. "Wait until you see dessert."

"I'm drooling already."

He laughed and dug into his salad. "In all the excitement, we forgot lunch."

She thought about that. "Huh. I guess we did."

"You wouldn't notice because you're a two-meals-a-day person. But I was starving."

"Yet you waited for me."

"I am a gentleman."

She laughed and tasted her lemon arugula salad. "So good."

"That's another thing I like about you. You're not afraid to eat."

"Not when I'm hungry."

They finished their salads, ate the chicken marsala and groaned with pleasure over chocolate cake with raspberry syrup. Then he took her hand and invited her to dance in the moonlight by the pool. The quartet played softly in the background while they nestled together, enjoying the evening breeze and each other.

The time for talking had ended with their meal. The fantasy of being the only two people in the world took its place as they slow danced to the soft music. She wouldn't let herself think about tomorrow or her troubles. She wouldn't let her thoughts drift to where he might be this time next month. Tonight, he was hers and that was all that mattered.

It was also enough to get her to tilt her head a bit so she could kiss him, softly at first, to not disturb the mood. But as the kiss continued, it took on a life of its own, deepening, and filling her with pleasure-induced boldness.

She smoothed her hands down his back as his hands found the closure of her dress. Surprised, she pulled back. "We're not alone."

"Yeah, we are. Listen."

She realized the music had stopped. She'd been so engrossed in the kiss she hadn't noticed.

She smiled at him. "But I'm supposed to be seducing you."

"I'd say we've always been seducing each other."

That made her laugh. He kissed away the sound in the darkness, as he undid the catch of her dress and let it puddle to the patio floor.

"You're barefoot."

"I know." Basking in her boldness, she undid his tie, then all the buttons of his silky white shirt.

Standing in the moonlight in only panties had to be the most decadent thing she'd ever done, yet a sort of rightness filled the tropical air, along with the sound of waves caressing the shore.

He looked around. "This place isn't made for first times when everything has to be perfect." He caught her hand and led her inside to the room across the hall from hers. He didn't close the door, just pulled her to him and began kissing her again.

It had been so long since she'd been held, touched, that a reverent feeling stole through her. It tried to sabotage her courage, so she took a breath, stepped away and gave him a nudge that knocked him to the bed.

But he caught her hand and tugged her with him. He kissed her, lowering her to the soft comforter. Everything was special, perfect, but she wanted the fun. She wanted the freedom. With another bump to his shoulder, she rolled him to his back and took control of the kiss. She liked this guy, and he liked her. The pleasure of that alone intoxicated her.

Her hands roamed his chest, while his found her breasts, then slid to her bottom. They'd been building to this from the minute she'd met him, but the fruition of her dreams was nothing compared to the reality of touching him and tasting him.

Her tongue drifted down her torso, but stopped when she found a long, thin scar. Reality stumbled through her. He'd been hurt. Nearly killed. But without that accident and an unexpected four years of being off the grid, she never would have met him, never had this wonderful space of time when he was just hers.

Emotion spiked. The memory of how fleeting

life was mixed and mingled with the knowledge that in this moment he was hers.

They came together in a roar of desire. Tingling with arousal, she groaned with need as their passion set the world on fire. None of her past relationships had ever felt like this. But she was glad. Grant was special. Now, in her memories, he would always be.

Afterward they lay nestled together. His arm beneath her shoulders, he stroked his fingers down her bicep.

"You know what?" he said, pulling his arm from beneath her. "I'm getting the champagne."

She sat up. "Good idea."

He returned with a new bottle, popped the cork and poured a glass for each of them. As he sat on the bed again, he shook his head. "Has anyone ever told you how perfect you are?"

"You mean, physically? That's just the good luck of mother nature. And it's nothing more than symmetry. Everything is proportional and balanced."

He leaned forward and kissed her. "Yeah, well, I love your symmetry."

She giggled at his silliness. "And there are parts of you I also love. Actually, you're just about physically perfect too."

"You saw the scars. I'm not perfect."

Laying her hand on his cheek, she held his gaze

to make sure he knew she meant what she said. "You're more perfect than you think."

He leaned·in and kissed her again, softly, as if thanking her for her confidence in him, but this time he didn't stop. As if he couldn't get enough of her, he kissed her until arousal rose, and the champagne glass in her hand felt clumsy and unwanted. They might have just made love, but she hadn't lied when she said he was more perfect than he thought. Everything about him appealed to her—even his scars. His accident hadn't just changed him; in some ways it had made him whole.

She warned herself not to make a big deal of how wonderful and perfect he was to her. She had to bring herself back from expecting too much or even wanting too much. This was a fling. That was the one thing she knew for sure. Each of them had lives to·work out. This time next month, she'd be in Montana.

In a way, she really was Cinderella. When their time was up, their affair would be over. They would go their separate ways. She had to enjoy him now.

She pulled back, took a sip of her champagne then set her glass on the bedside table. She took his glass and set it beside hers.

"I'm sensing you have a plan."

She nudged him enough that he fell back to his

pillow, then she straddled him. "Just appreciating the moment."

"Which is exactly what I wanted. A little time away to enjoy ourselves."

She kissed him to shut him up.

He laughed against her mouth, and she saw it: the thing that made their being together perfect. They weren't taking themselves too seriously. And both loved to laugh. To savor. To enjoy.

She spent the next five minutes showing him just how much there was to enjoy, then he rolled her over and joined them again. Pleasure intensified until she wished, if only fleetingly, that this could never end.

But she didn't let the notion stick. They had things to do. Lives to gather up and restart. When his autobiography was done, they would go in different directions and probably never see each other again.

CHAPTER TEN

THEY WOKE LAZILY the next morning. He kissed her soundly, then got out of bed to use the bathroom. When he returned, teeth brushed and face splashed with warm water, she was gone. But she slipped into the room a few seconds later.

"I thought it would simplify things if I used my room."

He caught her to him and kissed her. Even the few inches shorter she was than him somehow made everything about her sexier. They made love again then showered together before dressing in shorts and lightweight tops.

In the great room, he pointed to the open doors. "Walk on the beach?"

"I think I'd like to tour the common area of the resort. We woke so late we didn't have breakfast. I'd love lunch."

He put his arm around her and directed her out the folding doors. "Whatever you want."

They walked along the shore until they reached the public beach for the resort. Men and women in colorful beach attire sat on blankets or chairs, reading, chatting and enjoying the day. He directed Lola to cut to the path leading to the resort and entered the space with doors folded open to give the place an outdoor feeling.

They ate lunch, swam, had another private dinner and another amazing night together. But time slipped away too quicky and suddenly it was Sunday morning. Lola slept so soundly he hated to wake her, but he couldn't seem to leave the room. He almost couldn't believe she would go back to Montana, and he'd probably never see her after that. Even if she came to his island to decompress after the sale of her ranch, he wouldn't be there. He'd be in a city, starting his new company.

He also couldn't ask her to move with him. Wherever he was going, his life would be chaotic. No matter how good his intentions, he wouldn't have time for her. She'd be alone most of the time. That would inevitably result in a breakup that would hurt them. He'd already played out this scenario with one wife. He didn't need to repeat it with a woman he adored.

It was better to simply let her go—restart *her* life.

Still, his chest hurt when he thought about her departing his island, saying goodbye to her—and mere days later handing Max off to two strangers in France. Trying to assuage the awful ache, he got out of bed, grabbed his phone and headed to the kitchen. He made a single cup of coffee and walked out to the patio. With a few clicks on his phone, he called Caroline.

When her face appeared on the phone screen, he said, "Is Max there?"

"Yeah, they're eating cereal in front of the hotel TV. Then we're going to head south, back home again." Her eyes lit. "How is *your* trip?"

"It's great. The break we both need from the book. The place is perfect. Beautiful. Sinfully luxurious. I'm going to have to give you a few days at this beach to thank you for being so good to Max."

"Max is a pleasure to have around." She laughed. "But book me a whole week and I'll call us even."

He snorted. She was a better negotiator than he was some days.

Max walked into the camera view. "Hey, Max!"

"Hey, Dad!"

Caroline gave him the phone.

"Are you having fun?"

"Busch Gardens is awesome."

He laughed at Max's incessant use of *awesome*. "No kidding. Lola and I will be back late this afternoon. Caroline says you guys are starting home now. You'll probably get there before us."

"Okay."

He smiled. "See you soon," but he suddenly envisioned himself only having phone conversations with his son, who would be across an ocean. With the time differences, they'd have to schedule their calls—

His mind rebelled at the idea that their contact would be so limited and frustrating. He silenced it. Though he'd met Pierre at the memorial service, he hadn't contacted the Rochefort couple yet to talk about Max. Plus, he had to be honest about what his life would be like after he set the wheels in motion to produce the ideas he'd been working on the last year. His days would be filled with meetings. He'd need office space, employees—

Hell, he'd have to pick a city before he could produce the products he envisioned. It amazed him that no one had thought of these things, or even accidentally stumbled across the software tools that so obviously filled needs. But if there was one thing he'd learned about his brain, it was that he saw things differently. It was a blessing and a curse. But it was also a gift. Something he had to use. He could see the future. He had the talent and imagination to bring that future to life. That was his purpose.

And he'd seen Max catch Pierre's hand at Samantha's memorial service. Max loved him.

He said goodbye to Max, then took a solid breath, telling himself to stop thinking about the future. He'd never before whined about the responsibility of having talent. Yet, this morning, in the soft sunlight, watching a glistening pool, he wanted nothing more than to be lazy, to take long weekends at resorts, travel—show Max the world—and work, but not at such a frenetic pace.

But he knew himself. He knew that once he started working again, his life would be absorbed. He wouldn't stop when eight hours had passed. He pushed harder at nights. He did the work. He got things done—

Because that's how he worked. Full-on. Every cell in his brain engaged.

He wished it was otherwise. He wished he could punch a time clock and work like a normal person.

But he couldn't. He'd already been through this with his first company. If there was one thing he'd learned from that experience, it was to accept who he was and use who he was to make the world a better place.

He had three weeks to soak in everything he could and establish a relationship with his son that would survive living apart.

Then responsibility demanded he break away and do his duty.

Lola opened her eyes to find Grant giving her a slight shake.

"We have a limo coming in forty minutes."

She groaned and closed her eyes again. "Already?"

"Sorry. I've been up for two hours. I video chatted with Max who had fun but clearly is ready to come home. That means we need to be there too."

"Damn it. That's probably the only thing you could have said that would keep me from begging for another day."

He leaned down over the bed to kiss her. "We can come back, you know."

She still hadn't opened her eyes. "Promise?"

"Absolutely." But unless they stole away for another few days before the book was finished, he knew that was wishful thinking. He didn't say it. He refused to destroy the spell they'd been weaving. It would break soon enough on its own.

Returning to her room, she showered and dressed, then packed her duffel and overnight bag. Hotel employees came around to gather them and Grant instructed them to bring the three dresses from the closet.

"I bought them," he said, scrolling through his phone. "You never know when we'll want to play dress-up at the house."

She laughed and headed out to the limo as the resort employees packed it with their things. They took the boat to the island with the airstrip and got into Grant's jet. After a flight that felt far faster than the one to the resort, they were back in South Carolina, where they took another limo and another boat and arrived at Grant's dock to find Max waiting for them.

As soon as Grant stepped on the gray boards,

Max launched himself at his dad, hugging him around the waist. Grant stooped down and caught him to his chest, giving him a proper hug.

Lola imagined that Grant and Max probably hugged when Grant put him to bed, but she'd never seen them so filled with emotion over being together again. The sight stole her breath. There was no denying their connection. But there was also no denying that all their problems—especially the knowledge of a future spent apart with Max on another continent—surrounded them.

She would be leaving before Grant took Max to visit his French cousins. But the father/son separation was coming too. Because Grant was re-entering his real world. And she had to re-enter hers. Get a job. Support herself. Sell her family home—

"Lola?"

She brought herself back to the present. Then Max hurled himself at her, hugging her waist. Her heart slid to her throat. Love emanated from him, along with heartfelt joy.

"I missed you guys."

Grant slipped his arm over Max's shoulders. "We missed you too."

"Me too," she said, her voice a hoarse whisper. No matter how wonderful those two days had been and how wonderful the next few weeks could be, this was not her life. She had no permanent place with Max and Grant.

A little voice whispered through her brain. *Are you sure?*

Of course, she was sure.

Once you sell your ranch, you're free to do what you choose. Stay here. Find a job in the city where Grant settles.

And what if Grant didn't want her for anything more than a passing fling? They'd both gone into their relationship knowing it would end.

She also knew Max loved his cousins. His voice rang with it every time he talked about them. He'd hugged Pierre. Taken his hand at the memorial service. There was more to his life than either she or Grant knew.

The three of them together was temporary.

But what if it wasn't?

The persistent argument in her brain annoyed her. How dare her thoughts nudge her to reach for something that couldn't be? Still, she looked around, really saw the easy love Grant had for Max and Max had for Grant, as she remembered the intensity of the feelings she and Grant had shared in the Caribbean.

What if you're the glue that makes it possible? What if yours is the voice Grant needs to hear?

The thought stopped her. She wouldn't let herself even consider that they could stay together. Or that she was the person who made it all work. Or that hers was the voice of experience Grant needed to advise him.

She'd lived through the loss of both of her parents. She knew the upcoming separation would be more heartbreaking than Grant could imagine. Grant had a child he clearly loved. And Max might have lost his mom, but he and Grant had bonded. Still, Grant's experience with his parents wouldn't let him see that family, blood ties, were not something to be taken lightly.

He and Max needed each other. Yet he was letting Max be raised by someone else so he could go back to work.

It suddenly seemed all wrong.

What if Grant sending Max to Paris was wrong and what if hers was the voice he needed to hear about *that*?

What if that was her place here? Telling him to take the first step of keeping Max, so they could take all the other steps that came after?

Heading to the patio door with Max, Grant faced her. "Coming?"

She looked at the little boy, the tall man. A new future popped into her overly busy, overly optimistic brain. She could see herself living here with Grant and Max. Making friends. Making a real life like the one she'd had in her small town growing up. Christmas. Siblings for Max. Bedtime stories. Manic breakfasts as everyone tried to get out the door for school and work.

Oh, God.

It made perfect sense.

Except Grant needed to go back to work. And even if he found room for Max in his life, *she* was the one for whom there was no place. His marriage and divorce had taught him that.

Plus, he'd said what they'd had was temporary. Wouldn't she be foolish to believe there might be more for them and have him tell her he didn't want her?

CHAPTER ELEVEN

THE NEXT MORNING, Lola awoke to noise and confusion. She'd slept in Grant's bed, but he was nowhere in sight. She slid out from under the silky sheets and into the clothes she'd worn the day before so she could sneak up the flight of stairs to her room, quickly shower and dress for the day.

When she walked out of her suite wearing shorts and a T-shirt, with her hair in a ponytail, the noise greeted her again. It sounded like ten people all trying to talk over each other. She followed it to the dining room where Grant and Max were having breakfast with an older couple—

Grant's parents.

She'd seen their pictures several times when she'd gathered data for his autobiography. His father was tall like Grant, but he had fair hair and blue eyes. While Grant got his height from his father, he had his mom's coloring. Dark hair. Dark eyes.

His father rose as she entered the dining room. "No need to stand for me. I'm hired help."

His father chuckled as he sat again.

Grant said, "Mom, Dad, this is Lola Evans, the ghostwriter Gio hired. Lola, these are my parents Ron and Teresa."

His mother gasped. "Oh, it's so nice to meet you! Everybody gets everything about our Grant wrong. He's the nicest guy in the world."

Grant frowned at his plate. Not as much as glancing at either parent, he said, "Mom. I'm not nice. I'm a dictator when I work. I'm gonna own that."

Teresa snapped open her napkin and set it on her lap. "You're supposed to be a dictator. You're the boss. You know what needs to be done and how to do it. Your job is to get others to do what you say. Sometimes that means being strict or difficult."

Lola blinked. Wow. The about-face from how nice Grant was to the assertion that he was supposed to be a dictator left Lola's head spinning. But hadn't Grant warned her his parents were workaholic physicians who had affairs and left their children to their own devices?

Deciding to tread lightly, she took her seat and politely said, "It's nice to meet you both too."

Grant's dad said, "So what's the scoop? When's this thing going to be done?"

"We have a very narrow timetable," Lola said, peering at Grant to see if he was signaling for her to not say anything more. He wasn't. His attention was on Max, even though his father had asked a question.

She smiled at his parents. "I hope to be done this week in order to get two weeks of editing in."

His father waggled his eyebrows. "Anything juicy in there?"

Grant rolled his eyes and looked away.

Again, Lola replied. "It's a very straightforward story," she said, answering the question without really saying anything. "Your son's a hard worker. It comes through in the book."

His mom beamed with approval. "That's great." But her comment went unanswered. The table grew silent.

Grant's dad shifted a bit as Denise served his breakfast. When she pulled away, he said, "We're going to swim with the boys this morning."

Lola said, "You are?" then peered at Grant again.

He thanked Denise when she served his bacon and eggs. Then he said, "Caroline will be with them too."

Lola nodded and attempted to smile as everything tried to knit together in her brain. Grant not talking, insisting Caroline be with the boys when his parents could be watching them—

Grant wasn't merely holding himself back from talking. He did not trust his parents with Max.

It seemed extreme, except being a parent was new to Grant, and he clearly hadn't liked the way his parents raised him.

Denise brought Lola a plate of bacon and eggs and fried potatoes as she'd made for everyone

else. As if nothing was wrong, the elder Laninghams told story after story about their yacht club
and card club and the events they attended.

"Last year we went to the Kentucky Derby,"
Ron said. "Best time we've had in forever."

When Grant said nothing, Lola said, "It must
have been wonderful."

Grant tossed his napkin to his plate and rose
from the table. Facing Lola, he said, "I'll be in
the office."

Then he walked out.

After another ten minutes of listening to the
Laninghams, Lola finished her breakfast. Caroline arrived with Jeremy and shooed the boys upstairs for Max to get into his bathing suit.

Then she faced Grant's parents. "Grant texted
and said you'll be swimming with us."

"Yes. We were hoping to stay a few days but
with the autobiography and all, Grant said he
needs the privacy."

Lola said nothing, still trying to work all this
out in her head.

Clearly softening the blow, Caroline smiled and
said, "Yes. He's very busy."

Lola rose from her seat to go to her room to
gather the things she'd need to work with Grant.
Facing his parents, she said, "It was nice to meet
you."

Looking clueless, they both smiled, nodded
and said it was nice to meet her too.

She left the dining room shaking her head. Either his parents were so clueless they were delusional—

Or they hadn't been expecting a warm reception?

It bothered her enough that she almost asked Grant about it when they went to his office to work. Instead, she noted the fine aura of tension that surrounded him. He'd had enough stress for one morning, so she led him back to the discussions of creativity, a topic he seemed to love.

That afternoon, she watched him listlessly wave goodbye to his parents as Jason drove them back to the mainland to catch a flight to Key West.

Her story took another turn. Except it might be another one of those things she wouldn't be allowed to use. He hadn't forgiven his parents for ignoring him and his sister. He'd thanked them for paying for his education. He'd accepted that their version of love wasn't effusive and warm. But he hadn't forgiven them for his childhood.

It seemed petty for a guy who always thought in terms of logic.

But thinking about her own childhood, she knew it was the bonds she and her parents had formed over daily things—doing dishes, making popcorn and watching TV together that filled her with love for them and brought her home after every assignment to share the joy of her career.

If they'd been cold, or distant, or made her feel like she wasn't as important as their jobs and their charity work, she'd be a very different person right now.

And that was the part of the story she knew couldn't make it into the autobiography, even though it explained a lot.

A few days later, Grant and Lola were discussing the fact that they were very close to a final draft. They'd closed in on everything but his decision to go back to work. This morning he'd tell her that segment of his story, then she would not only put it into the book chronologically; she would also smooth out the sections where it affected the overall story.

Otherwise, the manuscript was strong. The book was just about done. Even as a nonwriter Grant could see that.

But while he was grateful that his autobiography was close to being done, he also knew that sending the manuscript to Gio meant Lola could leave. He didn't want to think about it, much less actually talk about it, so when his phone rang and Charlie's name came up on caller ID, he stopped to take the call.

Setting his phone on his desk, he said, "It's the PI I hired to check out Janine and Pierre." Then he hit the button to put the call on speaker. "Hey, Charlie!"

"Hey, Grant! I finished the deep dive that you asked me to do on Janine and Pierre Rochefort."

"Spill it."

Grant listened as Charlie rattled off details of Janine and Pierre's lives. Though Lola appeared to be looking at her notes, he knew she was listening too.

Janine was a well-respected lawyer.
Artist Pierre seemed like a kept man.
No gambling.
No alcoholics anonymous.
Bills paid on time.
Neighbors loved them.

Even with that information, Grant still had itchy feelings about Pierre but that was because he didn't really know anybody who didn't have a job except his ex-wife after she married him. And the impressions she'd given him were not positive. But he forced himself to see that it was good that Pierre didn't have to be somewhere every morning at nine o'clock. He painted in a studio in a small building in their backyard. He would always be around for Max.

Max would always have someone. He wouldn't be alone. He wouldn't feel like an annoyance or a problem.

This was for the best.

"I guess the next move is mine."

Charlie chortled. "I guess it is. If you need anything else, you know where to find me."

Grant disconnected the call.

Lola caught his gaze. "What was that all about?"

"After we met Pierre at the memorial, I called Charlie. Pierre seemed like a nice enough guy and Max clearly knew and liked him." He winced. "But I've been rich too long. Before I retreated to this island, I had a battery of lawyers who fought all the frivolous lawsuits brought against me just because I have money."

"Really?"

"Do you know how many hit-and-runs I was supposedly in? People believe I'd rather settle than go to court…so I hired a bunch of lawyers willing to take people to court for the things I hadn't done. I refused to be an easy mark for con men."

"I guess that makes sense."

"Because I'm used to people seeing me as a cash machine, I wanted the lowdown on Pierre and Janine. I didn't want Max living with them if they only saw him as a meal ticket—since I'll be paying child support and for anything Max wants. I also needed assurances that they weren't drug addicts or gamblers or even workaholics like me."

She took a second to think that through and for once didn't question his choice. Or ask for more information about his choice. Or demand his reasoning. She'd met his parents. If she couldn't understand his decisions about Max after that, she never would.

A few seconds went by, then she simply said, "Okay. Now what?"

"Now, we finish the book." And enjoy Max for the rest of the time he had before he began his quest to return to work in earnest. He felt the same way about Lola. Their time together was running out. He wanted every second of that too. The best way to get it was to keep working on the book, not turn it in early and have her leave. Not fly to France with Max and lose the child he'd only met a few weeks ago. But greedily hang onto this time.

He fought the sadness that threatened. Not because it surprised him—personal problems had never before interfered with his work—but because they still had almost two weeks. No one was taking the time away from him. Even if he had to think of creative ways to stall, he would.

"You're not going to call them?"

"My lawyers will make first contact. Then Max and I will fly to France together. I'd rather talk to them face-to-face, really see the relationship dynamics, make sure this is what *Max* wants before we discuss anything."

She hesitated but eventually said, "I guess that makes sense, too."

He sighed. "Look, I know you don't want me to give up Max. You don't even have to say it. But I've thought about this every way I could, and I know Max would be the one to suffer if I made the wrong choice."

She took a breath as if she were about to argue, but he saw something change in her eyes before she said, "Okay."

"Okay," he said, ready to get them back on track. "What were we talking about?"

She consulted her notes. "The day you decided to go back to work."

He laughed. "I didn't actually *decide* to go back to work. It was more like my brain woke up and started spewing ideas at me." He shook his head. "It was odd. I'd spent years like a hamster on a wheel, waking up, doing the stretches I had to do to be able to get to the dining room for breakfast, then swimming—which always loosened me up—then spending time on real therapy with two physical therapists, and then swimming again. Tired in the afternoons, I'd actually nap. Evenings I'd watch the Lions. Read. Keep up with friends. Then go to bed and do it all over again the next day.

"Work never entered my thoughts. I don't think I had the mental energy for it. Therapy is exhausting. Then one day I started thinking about artificial intelligence."

Her somber expression shifted to excitement. "Oh…that's interesting."

"I'm not going to tell you what I came up with. That's not going into the book. What I can say is that things just started connecting in my brain. What if this did this? What if that was expanded? What are practical applications?"

"And you came up with things?"

"Yes."

She stopped writing and studied him. "It must be amazing to see what's next before anyone else does."

"It's a blessing and a curse. But don't put that into the book. This is just us talking."

She nodded.

"Change is like a wave. Think back to your first cell phone. I'll bet you didn't have it long before you got a better one. Then smartphones came on the scene and suddenly we had enough power in our hands to see the people we called, listen to music, research anything, make videos of our lives, read books, craft a novel, take courses online, do our banking, bill clients—all with something that fits in the palm of your hand. It didn't happen overnight, even though it felt like it to consumers. But behind all that technology were the people who saw the possibilities and couldn't rest until they figured out how to make it happen. They didn't eat. They rarely slept. They couldn't. Work wasn't an obsession. It was more that discovery and implementation are intoxicating. There's an odd bit of fear in there too. With your brain popping with answers, you can't risk losing something—forgetting an option. You must act while the ideas are real and alive—before you forget them."

"Is that what's happening with you? That you have a million ideas that you're worried you'll forget?"

"No. I'm still in the possibilities stage. Once I start working, the practical application ideas will be like a tsunami."

She studied his face again. "It's going to take over your life, isn't it?"

"Yes."

"And you won't have time for Max at all, will you?"

They were back to the conversation that had begun after Charlie called. He didn't understand why she needed proof that his life was about to change, but now was the time to silence her doubts. "No."

Her expression shifted again. Her question became acceptance. "Then we really should make the best of these last weeks."

He caught her gaze and held it, assuring himself that she understood the truth of what he was saying. It wasn't just Max who was leaving. She would be too. He didn't want her to go. She didn't want to go. But they both knew she had to.

"We will."

Because he knew this time, these feelings, were what he would hold onto when he was running on adrenaline, working without sleep, connecting things and concocting things.

He returned to talking about how his thoughts built slowly, how he'd studied the current technology, read all the scientific papers written, delved into the dark web, listened to chatter and reconnected with the few people on the planet who could be called his peers.

He watched her expression as she realized he wasn't exaggerating when he said he wouldn't have time for Max—

Or her.

It hurt his heart to think about losing them, especially with their time running out, but if he held onto them, they'd be lonely and bored and eventually grow to hate him the way his first wife had. And he'd hate himself. Hate that he left them alone. Question his decisions. His commitment. Lose sleep over being disconnected and single-minded.

He'd hate himself for becoming his parents. He'd seen firsthand the damage they'd done by trying to be parents when their time had to be spent elsewhere. He would not ruin anyone's life because of his work.

It was better this way.

CHAPTER TWELVE

AFTER LUNCH, Max and Jeremy headed to the beach to throw a ball with Benjamin Franklin. Grant went to his office. Lola raced to her room to grab another notebook. She wouldn't let herself think about their discussion about Max that morning. Twice she'd almost argued with Grant, but both times she'd shut herself down. Not because this wasn't any of her business, but because Grant was a serious man who didn't take things lightly. He'd clearly thought this through.

Even if he was wrong.

Coming down the stairs, she groaned at the thought that insisted on haunting her. As much as her brain had told her she could be the voice Grant needed to hear, she did not trust it. She thought with her heart. Grant thought with his brain. She'd learned her lessons the hard way about listening to her heart. Hearts could long for things that couldn't be. Brains were a lot more practical.

When she entered Grant's office, he stood behind the desk, staring out at the ocean. Just from his posture she could tell something was wrong.

"Grant?"

He turned.

"What's up?"

"My lawyers called Janine and Pierre. They're ready for us to come to France whenever we're ready."

Lola tried to sound excited when she said, "That's great."

He said, "Yes. It is," but his voice was tired. And that little whisper about being the voice he needed to hear rose up again, so strong this time that she couldn't fight it.

She took a breath and said, "What are you doing? Why are you sending Max to France when you want to raise him?"

"I can't."

Desperation for Max filled her, and she understood why these thoughts wouldn't leave her alone. That little boy loved his dad and Grant loved his son. Surely, everything else could be worked out. "I say you can."

Grant shook his head. "You know what I think? I think your incredibly nice parents gave you a different perspective of life than what happens in the real world. If I raise Max, he will become the little boy who doesn't have anyone show up for his class plays or recitals or science fairs because I will have lost track of time and missed it. The question here isn't whether I should raise Max. It's whether I'm unselfish enough to see that he deserves better than me.

"Do you think I don't want him? That I don't want to watch him grow up?" He sucked in a breath and looked at the ceiling. "I do not want to hurt him the way my parents hurt me."

"They might have hurt you in the past. But I saw them jumping through hoops to get your attention or get you to talk the day they were here. And you literally froze them out."

"It was the best I could do."

"I get that. But your parents' openness and getting Max are like an opportunity for you to start over. Change your life. Have the things you never had."

He gaped at her. "No."

"Because you can't forgive them?"

He shook his head as if he couldn't believe they were having this conversation. "You're ghostwriting my autobiography. Yet, you haven't asked me why I never talk about my sister."

She frowned. "I assumed you didn't think she had a place in a biography that was more about your business life than your personal life."

"I never talk about her because she's dead."

Lola blinked. "What?"

"When your parents aren't ever around, you learn how to manipulate babysitters. It was so easy for her to sneak out at night by pretending to go to her room to study and then slipping out the back door. But more than that, we had absolutely no guidance. It was like our parents believed we'd magically mature as our bodies got bigger.

"Sneaking out to be with her friends led to other things. Eventually, she was a full-blown addict. She ran away because she couldn't hide it anymore. She also hated herself. Hated who she was. Had absolutely no self-esteem. When I found her years later, no matter how much I tried to help her she couldn't get herself together. Eventually, she was found dead in an abandoned building in Los Angeles. She had committed suicide."

Torn between sympathizing with him and confusion, she said, "How did I not find that when I researched you?"

"I had Gio bury the story. Not for me. Not for my parents. To give her a little dignity."

"I'm so sorry—"

"Thank you. But I've adapted. And she's finally at peace." He rose from his seat. "But let's just say I know the damage a bad parent can do. When I say I won't expose Max to that, I know what I'm talking about. I might have turned out okay—found my way without any guidance—but she didn't have a snowball's chance in hell."

With that he left the room.

Lola's breath shuddered in her chest. She didn't know when his sister had died, and she also had no way of finding out given that Gio had buried the story. But if it was around the time of Grant's meltdown when he fired half his staff, which resulted in his being kicked off his board, losing his marriage, getting hit by a car, that made sense. Her loss could explain Grant making mistakes, angering his board, and pushing his unsuitable wife to the point that she filed for divorce. It might also explain why his parents barely visited him around the time of his accident. He didn't *want* them around.

Dear God. That explained so much.

And that was probably something else she couldn't put in the book. Not if he'd had his sister's suicide covered up—for his sister. To give her some dignity.

Her heart ached. Tears filled her eyes. Grant had suffered a lot more than anybody would ever know.

Because he'd never let her put any of this in his autobiography.

That night, she slipped into Grant's room. After leaving his office without working that afternoon, he'd been sullen at dinner, but she'd thought he would return to the family room after putting Max to bed. She'd expected him to pretend nothing was wrong, make a pass, sweep her off to his room.

When he didn't, she showered and put on a pretty pair of pajamas and went there on her own. He was in bed, sitting up against the headboard, wearing navy blue pajamas and black frame glasses, watching a baseball game on the big screen TV on the wall that was usually hidden by a walnut cabinet.

She laughed. "What's this?"

"Maybe another slice of the real me. The only time I wear glasses is when my contacts are out, and I want to watch TV before I fall asleep."

She inched over to the bed. Without asking permission, she slid under the covers and eased her way over to him. Putting her head on his chest, she said, "I'm sorry."

He snorted but buried his fingers in her hair. "You're sorry? For what?"

"For making you talk. For pushing you when I shouldn't have."

"I just thought it was your aggressive reporter skills."

She took a breath. "No. Truth be told, I love seeing you with Max. I think you need him as much as he needs you…but I also see that you know yourself. Sometimes you're even brutally honest."

She pulled herself up and brushed a quick kiss across his mouth. He caught her elbows and kept her where she was, kissing her deeply, completely. The easy intimacy between them calmed her the way it always did. She'd never had a relationship like this, a person she could talk with so casually about the most important things. It might be because she'd been interviewing him for weeks and knew every corner of his life. Especially with his admission that day.

He was such a good guy, and he didn't see it. And it hurt her heart that he didn't.

She ran her palm against the soft top of his pajamas. "Oh… I like these. Let's take them off."

He laughed. "You, too."

"Race?"

He shook his head, kicking off his pajama bottoms with very little effort before he reached for the top. Without opening buttons, he caught the hem and pulled it over his head, tossing it across the room.

She wrinkled her nose. "I prefer a more mannerly approach."

He threw himself across the bed and yanked her to him. "You weren't very mannerly the other night."

"You bring out the best in me."

His deep-throated laugh filled the room and gratitude relaxed her a little more. She'd taken him to what had probably been the lowest point in his life that day, but she'd also brought him back just by coming to his room, being herself, accepting that their relationship was strong enough to handle the mistake she'd made by pushing him.

Love for him filled her soul, but she stopped it. What he'd told her about Max applied to all of his life. In a little over a week, she'd go home. She'd never see him again because their paths wouldn't cross. If she took him up on his invitation to vacation on the island after she sold her ranch, he wouldn't be here. He'd have already started his new life. She desperately wanted to enjoy him while she could, but she had to hold back her heart. Or at least keep her feelings in check.

Their kisses and caresses grew more heated, hungrier, and she felt the first crack in her armor. She'd never been as connected to anyone as she was to him. Even as she needed him, she wanted to be everything to him too.

She wouldn't let herself acknowledge that his work meant more to him than she did. That was an endless loop. She forced herself to be present, to enjoy making love, to sleep snuggled against him.

Try as she might to be happy, Lola had spent the next day miserable, knowing this wonderful life she'd begun creating was coming to an end. But there were two positives. First, these would be the best memories of her life. Second, her ability to connect with people had returned. Once she handled the sale of the ranch and found a new job, she would settle in a city where she would make friends. She could also reconnect with her old friends and bring them into her life again.

This wasn't the end. It was *an* end. But technically once she left this island, she would be starting a new chapter in her life. Actually, she'd be starting a whole new life, and in some ways, she believed she had Grant to thank for that. In others, she knew meeting Grant might have been a coincidence. She'd reached the point where it was time she moved on. He'd been in the right place at the right time to be part of it.

After only a few minutes, she stopped thinking of it from her own perspective, if only to force away the blues, and she focused on what was about to happen with Max.

Watching him playing with Jeremy and Benjamin Franklin, a few good ideas came to her for easing the transition. She didn't mention any of them to Grant until Max was tucked away in bed and Grant had come to the pool patio to find her.

"I was thinking maybe it might be a good idea for you to have Max call Janine and Pierre…you know. To sort of make a path for when you visit."

He shook his head. "I know this is going to sound selfish, but I don't want that interfering with the time we have left." He took a breath and expelled it quickly. "Besides, it's clear he knows them, clear they're close enough that they'll pick up their relationship as if there hadn't been a pause."

She nodded and dropped the subject. He hadn't shut her down because it wasn't her place to mention it. He'd stopped the conversation because he was feeling the end as much as she was. She heard it in his voice. He couldn't hide that from her now.

They had a little over a week and he wanted it, every minute of it. Even though another person might consider that selfish, she had come to realize Grant hadn't had a lot of love in his life. Was it so wrong for him to want to savor this?

No.

In the same way, she didn't want to think about the ranch she had to deal with when she returned to Montana. She didn't want to consider job possibilities. She didn't want to think about never seeing Max again. That would all happen soon enough. She wanted to breathe the salty air, bask in the sun, enjoy being with Max and make memories with Grant.

Period.

Because she could also see how much he wanted this life. How much it hurt him to give it up.

She caught his hand, pulling him to her so she could kiss him. For the first time since she'd begun interviewing him, she saw what other people called his selfishness as dedication. A burden he couldn't shake. She also saw how his parents' haphazard way of raising him, and losing his sister because of it, had bruised his soul. Out of necessity, he would be a long-distance parent, so he could allow his son to be raised by a couple Max knew and loved. His child would have love twenty-four-seven.

They kissed in the moonlight, making another

memory she could tuck away, then went back to the house.

He opened the bifold door, walked into the game room and twirled her around as if they were dancing. "Sleep with me tonight."

She laughed. "I sleep with you every night."

"I know. I just like asking and having you say yes."

He liked the assurance that she would be there for him. It was equal parts romantic and heart-breaking.

So they danced in the game room, then kissed their way to his second-floor suite and made love as if they didn't have a care in the world. As if they didn't know all this would end in the blink of an eye.

A week later, in the office, she handed him her three-hundred-page draft. "I'm emailing this to Gio this morning."

He glanced at it then up at her. "This is it?"

She nodded. "This is it. Your life. Every segment blended together. Every chapter a master-piece."

He snorted. "Right."

"Hey, that's my work you're snorting at. All you did was talk." She took a seat on the chair in front of his desk. "I have about a week before I get the copy-edited version."

"Are you being overconfident?"

"They said there wasn't time for a draft. There'd

be no content editing. This is my best work. Their editors will take a crack at finding holes or problems in the copy edit, but I don't think there will be many."

His eyes met hers slowly. Their usual sparkle was gone. He knew this was it. They hadn't even had a work session in days while she polished sentences.

"So you're leaving?"

"Honestly, I'd prefer to wait here for the edits and then to do them here."

He perked up. "My island is at your disposal."

"That's good."

He winced. "I'm not going to be around much. While you were polishing that thing, I've being doing video interviews with prospective employees. I have four more this morning."

"Are you sleeping with any of them?"

He frowned. "Virtually?"

She laughed. "I'm staying the extra few days because I like being with you, but I can swim with the boys and walk on the beach myself. The only thing I really need you for is at night."

He grinned. "You're the devil."

"Not even a minion. I like you. I'll take what I can get while we're waiting for edits."

His grin grew. The sadness disappeared from his eyes. "Sounds good to me."

"Okay. I'll email this, then I'll probably put on my swimsuit."

"I'll be talking to—" He reached for a paper on his desk. "Jim Billings, Josh Neville, Angel McDermott and Pete Farnsworth."

She walked around the desk and kissed him. "Sounds like I'm getting some real pool time."

He kissed her back. "Enjoy."

But when she walked out of his office, his grin receded. He was interviewing, beginning to choose staff. Gio had three prospective office spaces ready for him to see and choose from. Purely out of selfishness, he'd decided to locate his new company in Charleston, South Carolina. It was close enough that he could get back to his island in under an hour. He could still live in his beach house. Especially if he created a small apartment for himself in whatever space he rented for his offices—somewhere he could grab a nap if they pulled an all-nighter. It would be one less horrible shift he'd have to make in the big changes about to happen in his life.

When these interviews were done and he'd chosen office space, he and Max would be going to France to make the biggest change of all.

All this would be gone. Not just his son but the easy kisses and the real conversations with someone who liked him enough to challenge him—

He shook his head to clear it of the sadness and sense of loss and set up the first video call. Gio had sent him two piles of résumés. He'd weeded through them, choosing the best of the best. Then Gio had made first contact, because most people couldn't believe they were being contacted by Grant Laningham. They would dismiss email correspondence from him as a hoax or spam.

Once they agreed to an interview based on the company being created, its goals and mission statement, then Gio told them the company was being started by Grant Laningham. Half had declined based on Grant's reputation. Of the other half, he suspected a high percentage of them had only agreed to a video interview out of curiosity.

Which gave him about ten real candidates. But he only needed a handful of employees in the beginning. Once he got things off the ground, he'd find people as the workload grew.

Of the ten, he'd spoken with three already. He'd speak with the next four today and the final three tomorrow.

The first guy was a curiosity seeker, but Grant gave him enough information that by the end of their call he was excited for the project. The second candidate, a flashy woman with a PhD and tons of work experience with NASA, wasn't interested. The third guy ate an apple through the first five minutes of their hour-long call, but he was a decent candidate, so Grant kept him on the list.

The fourth guy was standoffish and questioned Grant brutally.

Eventually, the guy cut Grant off with a sigh. "This is a waste of time. I have a good job."

"I'm offering you a better one."

He had the nerve to grimace. "So, you say."

"You think I'm not smart enough to know my vision is revolutionary. That everybody involved will make money. That we'll potentially change the world?"

"You've been out of the game awhile, Grandpa."

Grandpa? What the hell kind of crack was that? "I was injured."

"Almost killed." He nodded thoughtfully. "I remember." He snorted. "Because I remember just about everything about everything."

For the first time in his life, Grant felt like he was getting a peek at what he must sound like to normal people.

"I've got a nice résumé and a cushy job. The only reason I took this interview was out of curiosity."

"Cushy jobs aren't cutting edge."

"I worked cutting-edge research and development once. It's not all that it's cracked up to be."

"Where were you working?"

He named a high-profile company. "I was developing a multi-universe game."

"Game?"

"System. The game could be whatever the players wanted, depending on their imaginations and skill set. You could play in one universe or seven. You could hone it down to your own city and your own enemies or you could try to rule a galaxy. The game could be a hundred different games. Meaning we had to plan for any contingency. Be smarter than any potential player."

"Interesting. I'm guessing you hated the long hours?"

"I loved the challenge."

Grant would have too. "So, what didn't you like?"

"The letdown when it fails."

That was interesting. And also explained why Grant had never heard of it. "Didn't you go through beta tests and get opportunities to fix things? How could it fail?"

"No real market. It was a thing of beauty, and consumers didn't want it. The people who did want it couldn't afford it."

Grant laughed. He found it hard to believe real gamers wouldn't have found the money for it. "Are you sure you weren't just in love with it because it was yours?"

"It was a diamond among coal in the video game world."

"That's too bad."

"No. It was poor planning."

"Probably." And poor marketing, if this guy was telling him the truth. "But I would think you'd want to clear your name. Show the world it wasn't you…it was management who failed."

"What?" His round face reddened. "You're challenging me?"

"I probably could. I could also probably teach you a thing or two."

He snorted. "Right, Gramps."

Grant's nerve ending shivered. He wasn't a babysitter or a mentor. He was a genius trying to find people to help him bring a vision to life. He didn't need an arrogant, angry pain in the butt.

"Okay then. I'll be reviewing my notes... You'll hear from Gio if you make the cut."

The guy said, "Whatever," and clicked off the call.

The guy had hung up on him, as if trying to insult him. Grant raised his eyes to heaven. Pete Farnsworth would have to work a little harder than that to insult him.

Still, when he left his office and went upstairs to get into swimming trunks, Pete Farnsworth's arrogance followed him upstairs and eventually outside to the pool.

He knew he'd been that arrogant as a newbie. He'd also created things that changed the world. That guy had nothing to be so self-important about.

Or maybe Pete Farnsworth wasn't self-important as much as he was bitter about having failed?

Grant didn't know. He also didn't care. The guy wasn't making the cut.

They swam that day and took Max to the beach

that night to play with glow sticks. The next day Grant interviewed another three people. Two very boring candidates caught his eye, if only because neither of them called him grandpa. They'd be great people to do the day-to-day grunt work required. And that's what he was looking for. People who could *execute* his ideas.

The next day Gio texted Grant to have Lola in his office in ten minutes for a video call. When they were all together, Gio gushed.

"I loved it. I wouldn't change a word. Copy editors are still going over it with a fine-tooth comb. The publisher is also insisting on fact verification."

Grant bristled. "It's my life. I know what happened."

Lola brushed it aside. "Fact checking is normal, Grant."

Gio said, "They want three more days."

Grant peeked at Lola then glanced at the computer monitor again. "Three more days?"

Gio winced. "Sorry about that. I know that cuts your revision time down to two days, Lola, but it was the best I could do."

She smiled. "That's fine."

Gio gushed a bit more then they signed off.

Grant laughed. "You called that one."

"I did. I saw the deadline and worked it all out in my head."

Grant's computer buzzed with another incoming call. A glance at the screen told him it was Janine and Pierre.

He and Lola exchanged a look before he answered it. "Hey... What's up?"

"We hadn't heard from you after we spoke to your lawyers," Pierre said. "We thought we'd check in."

"Everything's great."

Pretty blonde, Janine said, "You don't have any more information about when you'll be visiting with Max?"

He knew they were really asking if he was stalling. They didn't know about the biography, but technically it was done. They didn't know he'd begun interviewing employees to start a new company. They didn't know that the six he wanted to hire were enough to set up an office and get organized.

All they saw was a guy who'd almost accidentally gotten custody of his child—the child they loved. They'd told Grant's lawyers that because Samantha was alone, they'd always believed they'd be raising Max. Grant's lawyers had told them all that would be discussed when Grant and Max came to Paris.

And maybe the time for stalling was over.

"Actually, we could get on a plane tonight and be at your house around noon tomorrow."

Janine's face blossomed and glowed. "Really?"

He understood why. Max was a wonderful kid.

Pierre stuttered. "We can be ready for you any time."

"Good."

Janine said, "We'll see you tomorrow then."

Grant said, "Tomorrow."

When he disconnected the call, Lola gave him a confused look.

He sighed. "There's no point in putting it off."

She said, "Okay," and he suddenly realized she thought he was leaving her when they'd just gotten a lucky three-day extension.

"I want you to come with us."

"Oh."

"Have you ever been to Paris?" he asked enticingly.

She frowned. "Actually, no. I'd always said I'd attach a visit to Paris onto one of my assignments but never made it happen."

Their work done, he rose from his seat. "That's because you were always eager to get home to talk with those really great parents of yours."

She laughed and stood, too. "I was."

"So, come with us."

As he walked around his desk to stand in front of her, she took a breath. "This isn't going to be easy."

His voice softened. "I know. I'm not going to tell Max that he's staying until he's happily settled. Then I'll explain that I'll visit as often as I can and call at least once a week."

"Do you think you'll get time for monthly visits?"

"I think I'm going to hire an assistant who will force me to make time."

She laughed. "A bulldog?"

"I do like a good bulldog." He smiled and caught her around the waist to haul her to him. "You wouldn't be interested in the job, would you?"

CHAPTER THIRTEEN

It would be the perfect compromise. She could take the job as his assistant, make sure he ate and slept and put visits with Max on his calendar—refusing to accept any excuse for why he needed to cancel.

There would be no canceling visits with his son.

But she'd be a different kind of employee than the subcontractor ghostwriting his autobiography. She'd be in the daily grind of his work. She'd become part of a world that pushed him and punished him.

They wouldn't have any personal time. And even if they did, she could see their relationship deflating, turning into something that didn't have the life or romance it had here because of the confusion of working together. Their roles would change.

What they had would die.

That would hurt more than walking away now. At least now, they had good memories and a soft spot in their hearts for each other.

She pretended he was teasing. Maybe he was? "Oh, you wouldn't want me for an assistant. I'm accustomed to having assistants. And I'd bark at you."

He laughed, taking the tension out of the room, making her believe he really had made that suggestion as a joke.

"I'm the only one who gets to bark in the office." He kissed her quickly. "Thank you for coming to France with me. This *is* going to be hard."

She knew it was. She also saw that he finally understood just how difficult it would be. While that was good, understanding wasn't going to make things easier.

She followed him out to the pool where Max, Jeremy and Benjamin Franklin were swimming.

"Max, you want to come out here for a second?"

Max nodded and swam to the ladder. Unconcerned, Jeremy picked up the Frisbee and tossed it for Benjamin Franklin who eagerly raced after it.

Lola sucked in a soft breath. The boys had made friends. Benjamin Franklin's life had found a new purpose—

And this time tomorrow all of that would be gone. The pool would be silent. The dog would spend most of his days sleeping in the sun.

Grant sat on the edge of a chaise lounge. Lola sat on the one beside it. Max ambled over.

"What's up?"

"Lola and I have been talking to Janine and Pierre."

The little boy's eyes lit. Some of Lola's worry softened. She remembered how Pierre had hugged Max and Max had clung to Pierre's hand.

"We're going to fly to Paris tonight to see them."

Max's mouth fell open in disbelief, then he jumped for joy. "All right!"

More heaviness fell from Lola's heart. She watched Grant force a smile. "I'll have Caroline pack for you. Then I thought we'd all spend the afternoon on the boat."

Max nodded eagerly again.

Lola didn't wonder whether she should join them. Max was enthusiastic and that was great. It really did take away part of the worry about the choice to have Janine and Pierre raise Max. But Grant needed this.

An hour later, the warm sun lulled Lola into contentment as Grant and the boys put on life vests and jumped into the ocean.

"Hey, sleepyhead!" Grant called.

Max seconded that. "Yeah. Put on a vest and swim with us."

She waved her book. "The last time I was out on the boat I realized this would be the perfect place to read. I came prepared."

Grant shook his head. "Nope. Read on your own time. We're swimming."

Realizing this was a losing battle, she said, "Okay, but I don't need a life vest."

She dove off the boat into the water and surfaced beside Grant. He shook his head. "You really always have to do things your own way, don't you?"

She laughed. "Sometimes." She caught his gaze. "Does it bother you?"

"I think it makes you interesting."

Their attention caught by something shiny, the boys swam off. Grant watched them. "He's going to miss this."

Shielding her eyes from the sun, Lola said, "You could arrange for him to spend two months here with you in the summer."

"I can never really predict I'll have that much time off. But I see what you're saying. With the new office only about forty minutes away from the island, lots of things about my life could be more easily managed. But I'm just not sure I can be available for two months."

"You can't make a schedule?"

He glanced at her. "That's actually the point. Ideas and answers to problems come at their own speed. I could clear my calendar, and on the day he arrives for the summer, I could finally figure out something in my work and get so involved I don't come home."

Not wanting to go over this yet again, Lola said, "Well, think about it."

"I will."

"Good. Because if you could work that out, it would be the perfect way to be in his life. To help him to realize that you are his dad and you do love him."

Grant's eyes grew solemn and sad. "I do love him."

Which was why she'd agreed to go to Paris with him. No matter how difficult Grant believed leaving Max was going to be, she knew it would be a hundred times harder and he would need her to be there for him.

They boarded the plane for the overnight flight. Lola's suggestion of Max spending two months on the island had followed Grant the rest of the afternoon and through the drive to the airport. He loved the idea of having Max spend summers with him and would try to make it happen, but he wouldn't tell Max about it to prevent disappointment if he couldn't work it out.

Dressed in pajamas and tucked under a cashmere blanket, Max fell asleep first and woke first. When Grant yawned and stretched to wake himself, it was to find his son dressed in jeans and a T-shirt, sitting on one of the chairs by the table, amusing himself rolling the Yahtzee dice.

"Hey. What's up?" He glanced at his watch. Six o'clock in South Carolina. They'd been sleeping like rocks for hours. At least, he hoped they had. "Did you sleep?"

Max nodded eagerly.

"Everything okay?"

He grinned. "Yeah."

Grant suddenly understood. Max was eager to see Janine and Pierre. Staying at the island had been like a vacation. But his reality was that he'd lost his mother and the two people who were most like family to him were Janine and Pierre.

Max wanted to be with them.

Easing his chair in the upright position, quietly so he didn't wake Lola, Grant said, "Okay. I'm going to shower and get dressed too."

In the shower, he worked to shake off the feelings that tumbled through him as he acknowledged that Max loved Janine and Pierre and they were more family to him than Grant was.

Sliding into khakis and a polo shirt, he experienced the kind of emotions he'd never felt before. Any guilt or odd thoughts he might have had about allowing Janine and Pierre to raise his son disappeared, but they were replaced by his own sense of loss. He'd never in his life loved anyone the way he loved his son. And he couldn't raise him.

Still, the more important consideration was that Max loved his cousins and wanted to be with them. Grant's emotions didn't count, Max's were the ones that counted.

Grant didn't talk much on the drive to their home. He'd rented a car so he'd have transportation for the few days they would be in France. He knew he had to get Lola back to the States once the copyedit of his autobiography was returned. But he wanted to spend time with Max and Janine and Pierre to make himself a part of their family before he went home and lost himself in work.

They arrived at the French provincial style house in the country on what appeared to be acres of ground. Pretty gray and brown stone created a timeless look and feel of a country estate. The perfect place for a child to grow up.

Janine and Pierre ran out to meet them. Max threw himself into Janine's arms and she hugged him fiercely. "I'm so sorry about your *maman*."

Tears filled Max's eyes and Pierre took him from Janine to hold him. "We will love her forever and never forget her."

Max nodded. Pierre squeezed him tightly.

Janine glanced at Grant. "Can we help with bags?"

He shook his head. "We don't have a lot. I'll be shipping other things later."

She nodded her understanding that Grant didn't want to say too much in front of Max. He hadn't yet talked with Janine and Pierre about Max living with them. So he couldn't tell Max yet.

Pierre slid the little boy to the ground and took his hand. "We have new chickens."

Max said, "All right!"

Pierre and Max walked into the house and through the corridor to the kitchen of the open-floor-plan downstairs and out the back door.

Janine said, "He's taking him out to the coop."

Grant nodded stiffly. The house was perfect, a cozy family home. A wonderful place for a little boy to run with a big yard to play in and a chicken coop that Grant could see through the sliding glass doors leading to a perfect patio.

He shouldn't have been angry or negative and Lola reminded him of that as they whispered to each other in the darkness before falling asleep after an afternoon of getting to know Janine and Pierre and watching Max happily interacting with them.

The next day, Max played with Pierre in the backyard, painted with him and in general was like his sidekick. Midafternoon, Grant, Janine and Lola sat by a big window, having coffee, watching them.

"He's always loved Pierre," Janine said with a laugh. "You know, if you wanted to spend the rest of the day in the city, we wouldn't mind."

Grant's gaze stayed on Max. He was happy. There was no doubt about that. But he'd also been very happy on Grant's island. He didn't know how a kid could look so at home in two places, but Max did. For as much as Grant tried to adjust to leaving Max behind, he simply couldn't do it.

His eyes on Max, he said, "I think we'll just stay here."

Janine nodded.

They hadn't yet out-and-out discussed custody. No one had even hinted that Max would be staying with the Rocheforts when Lola and Grant returned home, but Janine's behavior almost indicated she thought it a foregone conclusion.

Knowing what he did about his work and parenting, and how happy Janine and Pierre were to have Max, this should be a no-brainer. He should want his son to have a secure, happy life with two wonderful people...but something held him back.

His phone buzzed with a video call, and he frowned. "I'm sorry. I have no idea who this is, but I have three potential office spaces to look at when we get home and six newly hired employees who might be getting cold feet."

"Go. Answer it," Lola said, batting her hand. "We're fine."

He walked through the foyer of the big house and into Janine's office. Closing the door, he clicked on the call only to have the face of Pete Farnsworth rise on his screen.

"Dude."

Grant frowned. Not just at the weird greeting, but he was fairly certain Farnsworth had hung up on their last call. "What do you want, Pete?"

"I was thinking about the job."

A crazy kind of hope rose in Grant. Pete Farnsworth had been the smartest, most experienced person he'd interviewed. He'd love to have him on staff. He could actually see himself freeing up some of his time by handing off some of the more difficult work to Pete. Which would translate to time for visits with Max.

But he didn't want to give that away. He said simply, "Yeah?"

"I've been thinking about the bits you told me about your new products, and I got some ideas. You don't need to pay me or thank me. I just like where you're going with the artificial intelligence stuff, and I want to share a few thoughts."

Grant blinked. "I can't take your ideas. My legal people would shoot me."

"I told you. You don't have to pay me. I just see all the potential—"

"I think you want to be part of this project."

Pete sighed. "I have the easiest job in the world. And I don't want to be your grunt. I'm a supervisor here. I'm staying. If you want my ideas, you know how to reach me."

With that he clicked off the call and Grant rolled his eyes. Technically, that was the second time Pete had hung up on him.

As he returned to the table in front of the window, Lola said, "Who was that?"

"Remember the kind of grouchy guy I talked to last week? Well, he had some ideas for my projects that he wanted to share."

Lola laughed but lawyer Janine's eyes grew huge. "Without any sort of agreement in place he was going to just *give* you ideas?"

Grant shook his head. "I told him my legal people wouldn't let me take his ideas."

"If you asked me," Lola said, "he wants in on the project."

"I know he does," Grant agreed. "But he has a solid job and the last big project he worked on failed so he was fired."

"No confidence," Janine suggested.

"He's got lots of confidence. And from what I dug up on him before I called him last week, he deserves to have it, but he's holding back because he likes his salary and easy hours. I'm not going to beg him or make promises. Life is sometimes about risk. He needs to either man up or get comfortable with the fact that his cushy job will never allow him to make a real contribution. That's why he wants to give me ideas. He wants a place at the table. But he doesn't want the risk."

"Well, that's his loss," Janine said.

Grant laughed. "You investigated me, didn't you?"

"No more than you investigated us."

"At least we both know we don't make decisions lightly."

Janine's eyes softened. "No. We do not."

Dinner was chicken legs coq au vin with salads and side dishes. Max ate as if he'd never eaten before. He teased with Janine and gazed at Pierre with adoring eyes. By the time the evening of playing the French edition of Pictionary was over, whether Grant liked it or not, he felt the push he needed to give Max the right life.

Still, it broke his heart when he took Max upstairs to watch him get ready for bed. As he was tucking him in, Janine, Pierre and Lola came in to say good night. Max happily said good night as if he was ready for a solid night's sleep, but when everyone headed for his bedroom door, he said, "Can you stay a minute, Dad?"

Grant smiled and returned to the bed. He sat on the edge as everyone trooped out and closed the bedroom door.

"Am I staying here?"

Grant's mouth opened, but nothing came out. Max's blue eyes were solemn and intense. The kid was just a little too observant. But this was also a conversation they needed to have.

"It's not a done deal. I haven't even really spoken to Janine and Pierre about it but we're all thinking about it."

Max nodded. "Oh… Because I don't want to."

That surprised Grant so much he blinked. "You don't want to live with Janine and Pierre?"

"I like them, but I never had a dad. Now I do. I want to stay with you. I want to have a dad."

Swallowing back a groundswell of emotion, Grant tucked the blankets around Max. "You know what? I never thought of that. I just looked at the big picture. With Janine and Pierre you'd have a mom *and* a dad."

"Pierre's not my dad. *You're* my dad."

Grant's eyes filled with tears. He hadn't had one inkling of how much those words would mean to him. "Yeah, and I like being your dad."

"And I like being your kid."

He pressed his lips together, giving himself a minute to compose himself but also to gather up every nuance of this moment so he would remember it forever.

"I like having you as my kid… My son."

Max grinned, happily, easily, as if they hadn't just had the most profound conversation of Grant's existence and that life was a simple thing. Maybe for Max it was. Or maybe Grant made life hard when it didn't have to be. He had no idea how this would work, but he did know he'd make it work. Because right now, nothing else in this world mattered except the opportunity to raise his son.

Still, just to be sure, he said, "You're saying you want to come home with me?"

Max nodded eagerly. "And Benjamin Franklin and Lola and Caroline and Jeremy and Denise."

Grant saw it then. The family he'd created. All this time, he'd known what he wanted, and he'd been building toward it. He just hadn't realized it.

He leaned down to hug his son and Max partially sat up to accept the hug.

"Okay, we leave tomorrow morning. Before we go, we'll talk with Janine and Pierre about you coming here for visits."

Max nodded again.

"And maybe we'll have them come to the island for Christmas or New Year's—"

"Let's make them come for Halloween."

Grant laughed and rose. He had no idea why Max had suggested Halloween, but there was no way he'd break the happiness of the moment. "That would probably be fun." He took a breath. "I'll see you in the morning."

"I'll see you in the morning, Dad."

He walked downstairs, returning to the living room where they'd been playing Pictionary and sat down with a sigh.

Astute and observant, Janine said, "What did he want?"

"To come home with me. He'd figured out that this trip was me dropping him off to live with you and he told me that he wanted to live with me." Because he liked having a dad. *A real dad.* And Grant liked being a dad. But he wouldn't tell anyone else that. That would stay between him and his son.

Pierre looked sad. "He doesn't want to live with us?"

"I'm sorry."

Janine surprised Grant by grabbing his hand and squeezing it. "Don't be sorry. He loves you. I could see it. And we love him, but he can visit us. *You're* his dad."

Grant rubbed the back of his neck. "That's approximately what he told me. And I told him that he could visit you as much as he wants, but also we'd love to have you come to the island for visits."

Janine said, "That sounds lovely."

"And I've always wanted to paint something from the States," Pierre said.

Confident in a way he'd never been before about anything other than software, Grant said, "We'll make this work."

They talked a bit more then Grant and Lola excused themselves to go to bed. When they were under the covers, she nestled against him. "You seem happy."

"I'm beyond happy. Remember how we talked about happiness once and I said I didn't believe it was a permanent state?"

She laughed. "Yes."

"And how I told you I thought your parents were the exception to the rule or some such thing?"

She laughed again. "Yes."

"I get it now."

She sighed with contentment as she cuddled against him. "I hoped you would."

"I do." He closed his eyes, savoring her softness. He wanted to tell her that with Max's life sorted out, it was time for them to talk about her staying, too. But he couldn't do that. Not only did he have no idea how he would make his life work now that he had a son living with him. But also, her life needed to be straightened out. For all he knew, their fling might have been just the moment of happiness she needed right now. Maybe after she sold her ranch and looked at her life, other plans could have more appeal.

Especially going back to work. At one time, she'd been an important voice in American journalism—

And she'd broken an engagement, left a man she loved, to have that career. Proof that she loved working, loved being her own person.

And proof that he shouldn't try to hold her back from restarting her life, from having what she really wanted.

No matter how empty it made him feel.

CHAPTER FOURTEEN

MAX AND GRANT were so happy, so content on the return to the island that Lola couldn't stop watching them. Caroline and Jeremy danced for joy when the cruiser pulled up to the dock. Grant had made a call to tell them the news about Max staying, and they had been thrilled. Even Jason whistled a tune as he grabbed their things and took them into the house.

Grant hugged Caroline. When she pulled away, her eyes were misty. "You know I will do everything in my power to facilitate things."

"Thank you. Gio found three potential office areas for my new company within forty minutes of the island. So all my time won't be eaten up in travel. But I still have to pick one. Also, about half the new staff is from out of state. I'm probably going to have to assist them with finding places to live."

Caroline laughed. "I have connections. I can help you with that."

Walking with Caroline, he headed off the dock toward the house. "After that we have to find a school for Max. And I was thinking about hiring a nanny—"

Standing on the dock, Lola continued to watch them. Jeremy and Max making plans to swim. The dog dancing around the boys. Grant talking to Caroline like the employee that she was, giving her assignments that would ease the transition from single Grant to single dad Grant who was also putting his new office in a city close enough that this island could remain his home.

A breeze ruffled her hair and she realized she was still standing on the dock, beside the boat. No one had missed that she wasn't following. Father and son were both still basking in the decision that Max would stay with his dad. Caroline had work to do.

Technically, Lola had work to do. She had to go over the copyedits. Then she had to go back to her ranch. It wasn't home but it was the next logical thing on her to-do list, as Grant would say. She needed to sell it and then find another job so she could also make a home the way Grant was.

Grant, Caroline and the boys entered the house through the entry by the pool patio. The door closed. She still stood on the dock.

Then her phone beeped. Seeing it was Gio, she answered it. "Hey, Gio."

"Have you looked at the copyedits?"

"We just got back from Paris. I'm still on the dock."

"Get to your computer, take a look, call me if there's anything troublesome."

"Okay."

"And by the way, when you look at your deposit for payment, it's going to be a little more than you expect."

"What? Why?"

"Grant told me to double your fee."

Her eyes widened and her heart stuttered. That was a lot of money. "What?"

Gio laughed. "If there's one thing you should know about Grant Laningham, it's that he appreciates a job well done. You were a star, Lola. We needed you and you came through. Thank you."

Confused and a little dazed, she took a breath. "You're welcome, but the original amount was fair."

Gio chuckled. "Never argue with a bonus."

Remembering her bills, she laughed. "I guess I won't."

She walked into the house a little shell-shocked. It struck her that Grant was paying her for more than the book. He was thanking her for the advice she'd given him and the way she'd helped him turn his life around. She could have thought that insulting, except she saw logical Grant's purpose. She'd helped him. So, he was helping her in the way she most needed his help.

No one was around as she climbed the stairs to her room. Taking her laptop out to the table on the deck outside her room, she looked at the copyedits. With everyone busy, she started checking the changes made by the editors and the comments in the margins. She worked through dinner and was still working when the sun set.

A little after ten, she pulled away from the work. She rolled her back and shoulders to relieve some of the tightness then walked to the kitchen to make herself a sandwich. The room was totally different with no one there. Not noisy and happy. Shiny and silent.

Not in the mood for an empty room, she took her sandwich with her as she looked for Grant. Seeing lights on the pool patio, she headed out but when she got to the pool, she saw Grant and Max sitting on a chaise. Grant pointed out constellations. Max nodded, enjoying his dad.

Something wonderful fluttered through her. Max hadn't simply needed his dad. Grant needed his child. They also needed this time together to bond for real. Now that they had chosen each other, chosen to live together as a family, things would be different. The next few weeks would be about sorting that out.

She took a few steps back, then turned and walked inside the house again.

The horrible feeling of being unnecessary filled her. With the autobiography done, there was no place for her. An odd hollow sensation flitted through her. Not just that she wasn't needed but that she wasn't a part of things.

Because she wasn't. Max and Grant were settling in. Caroline was taking over some of Grant's planning—

Denise cooked. A nanny would be hired.

And her troubles still loomed large in her mind. A failing ranch. An unsold house in Pennsylvania. Employment to procure.

It was time to go back to Montana.

That's why Grant had added the money. He knew she would be leaving. He knew she would need cash for a fresh start. Even if she sold her ranch at a break-even price, thanks to him, she'd have money for her fresh start.

Tears filled her eyes. He really did see everything.

Most of her clothes were still packed from Paris. She could easily leave tonight.

Sandwich in hand, she returned to the kitchen where a sheet with the phone numbers of all the household employees was tacked on a bulletin board. After calling the airline and getting a flight to Montana in the morning, she found Jason's number and dialed it.

"Hey. It's Lola. I'm sorry to be calling so late but I need to go to the mainland. I'm flying out early tomorrow morning—" Not exactly a lie. She did have a flight to Boseman in the morning, but it wasn't so early that she couldn't have spent the night. But she didn't want to stay. She didn't want to feel like extra baggage anymore, or worse, interrupt Grant and Max as they basked in the happiness of being together. "Is it possible for you to come and get me?"

"Sure. Not a problem. I'll be right there."

They hung up the phone. Lola went upstairs to put her computer in its carrier. She packed the rest of her things, then took her luggage to the front foyer. Jason arrived in fifteen minutes. She saw Grant intercept him, so she gathered her things and raced out to the beach in front of the dark dock.

"Here's my duffel, computer and overnight bag," she said to Jason. "I'll be there in a minute."

He nodded. "Okay. I'll be waiting."

As he walked away, Grant said, "You're leaving?"

"That's always been the plan."

His eyes softened with confusion. "Weren't you going to tell me?"

"Of course, I was going to tell you. Jason just got here a little sooner than I'd thought he would. I have a world of trouble to get back to—"

He put his hands on her waist, pulled her to him and kissed her. "Stay another day. The trouble will still be there."

Temptation nearly overwhelmed her. She loved his handsome face, loved his ideals, loved his intelligence—

But she'd seen what his work ethic had done to one marriage. Now, he had Max—who needed his attention more than she did.

"I can't. You know...don't put off until tomorrow what you can do today."

"More wisdom from your mom?"

"I think Ben Franklin said it first."

He laughed, given that his dog was also Ben Franklin. "All right I get it. But staying one or two days won't hurt."

Today it was one or two days but at the end of those days, would he coax her to stay some more...and would she be depriving Max as much as she would be shortchanging herself? She had to move on. Anything she had here was temporary.

"Really. I have to go. I've lived with my grief and the ranch and the mess I made of my life for too long. It's time for me to fix things too." She bounced up and kissed him quickly, but as he always did when she kissed him, he caught her arms and kept her to him, so he could kiss her the right way.

She let herself sink into the kiss, let herself enjoy it and memorize every sweep of his tongue because she never wanted to forget this. Then she pulled away and smiled at him. Her heart ached. Her soul shimmied with sorrow. But she wanted him to remember her happy. She wanted his thoughts of her to be filled with good times, not a struggle.

"Thank you for everything."

His eyes searched hers as if he couldn't believe this was the end. Finally, he said, "You're welcome. Offer still stands for you to come back to decompress after your ranch sells."

She smiled, and said, "I know," but she'd never return. What they'd had was a once-in-a-lifetime thing. If she came back, while he was working and too busy for her, she'd only sully the memories.

The temptation to kiss him again was so strong that she pivoted away before she could and raced to the boat. Raincoat over her forearm, umbrella in her hand, she jumped in on her own and settled in quickly so Jason could head out before she or Grant changed their mind.

She caught her flight in the morning. That flight connected with a flight that connected to a third flight that would take her to Boseman. On the third flight, a dark, quiet flight with very few passengers, she let herself cry. Not because she was sorry that she'd connected with Grant but because she would never find anybody else like him.

And she'd lost him.

Grant spent most of the night staring at a whiskey bottle. He wanted to drink. He would have appreciated the numbness the alcohol would have brought after only a few shots. But he had a son. *A son.* A little boy who had changed his whole world.

A relationship with Lola in addition to that was out of the question. Yes, he understood that Lola could have helped him with Max, but the worry was that he'd take advantage of her as a built-in babysitter and then she and Max would both miss him.

And he'd have another huge emotional failure.

Two if he counted Max.

His priority had to be his son.

But he would miss Lola. Ridiculously. Unlike his ex, Lola spoke his language. Smart, funny at all the right times, serious in the others, she had a personality that meshed with his. It wasn't just about sex with them. They'd had *that* connection.

Eventually, he left the pool patio and went to his room where ghosts of Lola haunted him. After an hour or so he fell asleep, but his alarm went off at six. Normally, he could have hit the snooze button, but he knew Max woke early.

He went to his little boy's room and discovered he was correct. Max was already gone. Probably in the kitchen, telling Denise how to make French toast.

Correct again, he found Max kneeling on a stool by the center island and Denise laughing over his breakfast order.

"A peanut butter sandwich and pickles?"

He nodded. "Sweet and sour. My mom always said that was a good thing."

Denise laughed again.

Grant walked into the room. "I'm not having peanut butter sandwiches and pickles."

Denise said, "Thank goodness."

"I want eggs," he said, knowing that might pique Max's interest. "And home fries and bacon."

Max said, "I like bacon."

"Hmmm. Maybe you want to change your breakfast order."

Max considered it, then said, "No. We'll just add bacon to the peanut butter sandwich."

He laughed. "Come on. Let's go to the dining room and give Denise space to work."

Max jumped off the stool and led Grant into the dining room. When Max settled, thoughts of Lola returned. He'd never told her he loved her, but he felt more for her than he'd ever felt for another woman. He had to have loved her and he'd never said it.

Regret swelled in his chest. She should have known that he loved her.

Denise brought their food and Max chattered about what he and Jeremy intended to do that day. At the end of his list of activities, he glanced around. "Where's Lola?"

Oh, Lord. In all the confusion of coming home the day before and her leaving, and him wishing he could have a shot of whiskey, he'd forgotten to tell Max that Lola had left.

He took a breath. "Well, she finished the book—" At least he assumed that's what she'd done after they'd returned the day before. "It was time for her to get back to her ranch."

Max perked up. "She has a ranch?"

"Yes, but she wants to sell it."

Max looked at him as if he were crazy. "But she could have chickens."

Grant laughed. The simplicity of his thinking was equal parts interesting and fun. "No. She has to get on with her life."

From the expression on his face, Max clearly had no idea what Grant was talking about. "She has to find another job."

"Find another book to write?"

"Maybe. But she used to be a reporter. One of those people on TV or the internet who goes to places where things are happening like wars or earthquakes and she gets the story."

Max's face fell. "She's going to war?"

Grant almost groaned realizing he was going about this all wrong, giving Max all the worst ideas. "No. I don't know what she's going to do but I assume she will go back to reporting."

Unfortunately, thinking about her going to war wasn't any more comforting to Grant than thinking of her alone on a ranch in the middle of nowhere, trying to figure out how to make ends meet or hoping a real estate agent could find her a buyer—

He took a breath to stop his worries. She was a capable woman and he'd doubled her salary. She would more than pull through this. She would sell the ranch and find a great job and have a wonderful, happy life—

With a normal guy. Because that was the real problem. Grant wasn't a normal guy. He was a genius who believed he had to use his talent for the betterment of humanity.

Jeremy and Caroline arrived as Max was finishing his pickle. The boys raced out of the room and up the stairs so Max could get his swimming trunks on.

"Lola left last night."

Caroline said, "What?"

"Book is done. She has a ranch she needs to sell. And she wants to jumpstart her career."

Caroline deflated. "I liked her. I'd *hoped* you'd realize how special she was and convince her to stay."

"I tried," he admitted. "But we both know that I'm going back to a job that will consume me and now I also have Max."

"She didn't want to be second fiddle? That doesn't sound like her."

"It isn't her. That wasn't how she felt. She just… I just… I would hurt her, Caroline. Her parents were murdered. She's lived off the grid for four years. She's finally ready to re-enter her world— wouldn't it be selfish of me to beg her to stay?"

Caroline looked at the ceiling. "I don't know. I just saw you two had something special and I believe when two people have something special they find a way to work things out."

"I hadn't been able to in my first marriage. I have no reason to believe I would now."

He left the room and headed for his office. A flurry of emails showed that most of the staff had accepted his offers of employment and were dealing with Caroline about housing, but he still had to look at the office space.

A rush of adrenaline poured through him as he rounded his desk. He did want to go back to work. But even as he thought of the enormity of his new projects he deflated. He might want to work but he didn't want to go back to that *life*. The price of it was high. All of his time. All of his brain. All of his energy.

And companionship. He would always be alone because he would never drag another woman into the life he would be re-entering.

He sucked in a breath. Like it or not, this was who he was. He had to accept it.

He called the real estate agent Gio had used and spent the day with him going through the three potential office spaces. He finally decided on a building after the manager agreed that he could turn the far corner into a small apartment with a bedroom and bath and kitchenette.

Paperwork in hand, he returned to his island and walked to his office to store the copy of the leases that his attorneys were currently reviewing. He slid them into a file folder and then a drawer. As he turned to leave, his computer announced he had an incoming call.

Thinking it was Janine and Pierre, he was surprised to see the face of Pete Farnsworth pop up on his screen when he answered.

"Pete?"

"Yeah. I talked with a lawyer who said it was a simple thing for you to get some sort of agreement drawn up. Like you and I will chat about your new projects, and I'll give you input for which I do not expect to be paid."

Grant laughed. Fate must believe he needed comic relief because Pete's persistence and insistence on giving him his ideas was funny.

"It's still a no."

"Look, man, the world wasn't built by one person and you're not the only genius around. I could do your job."

Grant knew he was arrogant, but that was a little beyond arrogant.

"And I'm not asking you for money. Just to be a part of things."

"Oh, I get that," Grant said. "But you don't want to come to work for me."

"I don't want to lose the sure thing I have."

"But you do want to be a part of how the world's changing."

"Yes. But you know my story. I failed my first time out. Helping you but not really working for you would be like a cushion from failure."

"While you kept your easy job."

"It's a living."

Unexpected empathy for the guy rumbled

through him. He remembered how it had felt working for the first software developer who had hired him. He remembered feeling hemmed in. He remembered the frustration of working for someone else. Especially when they wouldn't implement his ideas. He knew what it was like to be smarter than his boss. He knew what it was like to have big dreams and no avenue to pursue them. He more than empathized with Pete. He'd lived a big chunk of his life.

"Are you sure there's no way to resurrect that game of yours? Do you own any piece of it?"

Pete paused. "I didn't own any of it. But what does it matter now?"

"Maybe contact your old employer. See if you can buy the licenses."

Pete snorted. "I'm guessing they want more for it than I have."

"I could back you."

"Really?"

"I might make it a provision of employment. If I front you the money to get the license for your game so you could do some upgrades and release it yourself, then you have to come work for me."

That resulted in a laugh from Pete.

Grant rolled his eyes. "Look, I'm a master at figuring out what people want, and I can tell you two things. First, *you* want that game to succeed. Second, you want to be boss."

Grant glanced at his résumé and confirmed a

few things in his education and experience before he said, "How would you like to be *me*?"

"What?"

"I don't want to run the show anymore. I have a son now. But I still have all these great ideas. I want to explain my ideas to someone who will understand them and let that person run with them."

Pete's face fell. "What?"

"I'm hiring you to run my R&D. I'll buy back your game for you. I'll hire a CEO and a financial manager for the new company. All you have to do is create the products."

He sat forward. "Are you serious?"

"Completely. Like I said. I have a son. I just realized I want to raise him. That means I can't be at the office twelve hours a day or work seven days a week. I need somebody like you to translate my ideas into software and software into products."

Pete stared at him.

"I will come into the office, get progress reports, chair meetings where we'll brainstorm. I'll also manage the CEO and financial guy." He laughed. "This could be fun. Me running the show without all the work. You getting to infuse my vision with your ideas." He paused and held Pete's gaze. "Take the job. I'm giving you a chance to change the world and myself a chance to have a life. All you have to do is say yes."

CHAPTER FIFTEEN

LOLA SAT ON the front porch of her ranch house the next morning, sipping a cup of coffee, after a long meeting with her foreman. She'd explained that she intended to sell the ranch and told him to continue doing what they had been doing. The hope was that the new owners would keep him and the hands, the way she had when she took over the place, and she'd try to negotiate for that, but there were no guarantees.

There might not be guarantees, but seeing the expression on his face, Lola had decided right then and there that she *would* work that into the deal with the new owner—if a new owner could be found.

She sat back in her chair, uncomfortable in her jeans and T-shirt when she was accustomed to wearing shorts or a sundress. But she wouldn't let her mind drift back to Grant's island. Instead, she nestled her hands around her coffee and reminded herself to take it one day at a time.

The sound of an approaching helicopter interrupted her peace and quiet and she took a breath. Her real estate agent had said he'd be at her ranch first thing in the morning. And this was first thing in the morning.

She rose, finished her coffee as she walked into the house and back to her kitchen. She put the mug in the dishwasher before she went outside again and headed across the field to meet the real estate guy.

Her heavy boots easily navigated the wild grass that grew in the field by the bunkhouse. Head down, she pushed her way to the clearing where the helicopter had landed.

Twenty feet before she would have gone as far as she could and still be clear of the blades, she stopped. A guy jumped out and headed her way.

The closer he got the more she squinted. He looked like Grant.

He *was* Grant.

She stood frozen. He looked so different in jeans and a plaid shirt—and boots. Her beach bum was wearing cowboy boots.

She laughed, then her breath stalled. Their first goodbye had been difficult enough. She wasn't sure she would survive a second.

When he reached her, he grabbed her and twirled her around. He set her down, kissed her soundly and said, "You look like a cowgirl!" He tweaked her nose. "So cute."

She stared at him. The kiss had robbed her of

the power to think and reminded her of everything they had. But they'd been down this road. There was no scenario in which a life together for them worked.

"Don't think I didn't notice your boots."

He laughed. "When in Rome—"

"Why are you here?"

He tweaked her nose again. "I came here to bring you home."

Her heart stuttered. Didn't he know how much she wanted that and how hard it would be to turn him down again?

"You know I can't come."

"Because of selling the ranch? Max thinks we should keep the ranch. You know. Get some chickens."

She stared at him again. "What are you talking about?"

"Max loves chickens. You saw him with Pierre's chickens."

When she only gaped at him, he slid his arm around her shoulders and turned her toward the house. "Okay. Since you seem a little slow on the uptake, I'll catch you up."

The feeling of his arm across her shoulders was so right that she could have nestled against him. But he was acting as if their lives were simple, happy, easily fixed lives and they weren't. She couldn't pretend everything was fine.

"I was tossing the paper copies of my new leases

on my desk, when I got another unexpected video call from that guy Pete…the one who wanted to give me ideas for no money."

Confused about where this was going, she said, "Yeah, I remember him."

"This time he'd called me to tell me my lawyers could easily write up an agreement that would allow me to talk with him about my ideas and use them for no compensation."

"That guy was weird."

"No. That guy really wanted to work on the projects I'd told him about when I interviewed him. So, while he was talking, I figured out what he really wanted, something he couldn't refuse, the license for the game he'd created that had failed—and my job."

"Your job?"

"I hired him to be me."

Her face scrunched. "What?"

"It all fell into place in my head while he was talking. I'll be hiring a CEO to run things and an accountant to keep track of the money… So why not hire someone to manage the research and development team? Pete was a little shocked at first too. But when I explained that I'd work as much as I wanted and be hands on, but he would be in charge he was totally in agreement."

"Can you do that?"

"I just did."

"No. I mean can you stand back and let somebody else shepherd your products?"

He took a breath. "Yeah. Easily. I'm not a kid anymore. I don't have to prove myself. I know things take time. I know there is no prize at the end for the person who makes the most money or has the most accomplishments. I know that living is about being happy."

She stared at him.

But she still wasn't sure what his job had to do with her. She'd figured out before she left that she had to be careful with the position he relegated her to. Not that she didn't want to be a mom to Max or be the happy, lucky woman who slept with Grant…but she needed more.

She wanted *everything*.

"So what do you say?"

"So what do I say about what?" she mimicked because she wasn't going to be the one to make any suggestions. If he hadn't figured this part out on his own, then she couldn't go back with him.

"Are you coming home with me?"

She glanced at the ranch to avoid him seeing the hope in her eyes. She had such strong feelings for him that she couldn't believe he didn't have those same feelings for her. But she couldn't pull them out of him. They had to be real. Natural. Spontaneous. From the heart.

"Seriously. If you're dragging your feet because you'll miss this place, Max really thinks we should keep the ranch."

She turned so she could catch his gaze. "Really? This is about Max?"

"Well, yes and no. Even if I didn't have Max, I think meeting you might have steered me into realizing that I'd already been through my workaholic phase, and I wanted a life." He smiled and took her hand. "You are that life."

The hope that swelled in her stole her breath. "Really?"

"Yes. I've slept in with you. I've worked in the morning but not in the afternoon because of you. You make me romantic and spontaneous when the only thing I used to think about was work, finding the next big idea. And you've told me enough about your parents that you've made me believe there can be another kind of life. A better life."

She smiled at him.

He stopped a few feet shy of the porch and slid his hands around her waist. "I don't want to do this without you. None of it. Create a company. Raise a son. Figure out how to be normal. I want you with me because you make me better and I love you for it."

"You love me because I make you better?"

"I think I love you because you're you. Cute. Funny. Sexy. Wonderful."

It was the last part that made her believe him.

She didn't want to be a sidekick. She wanted to be his woman.

She rose to her tiptoes to kiss him. This time he didn't have to catch her arms to extend the kiss. She could have kissed him forever.

Breaking away, he smiled at her. "You're so much fun."

"No. I might be fun, but you're happy." She paused, thought it through then laughed. "I make you happy."

"And that's funny because…"

"You didn't believe in happiness."

He laughed. "I didn't but I was coming around."

"All you thought you'd ever be was content… and here you are… Happy."

He took a breath, looked at the sky, then looked at her. "I wasn't that bad."

"You were. You definitely were." She took his hand and led him to the porch. "And I'm going to see to it that you never feel that lost and lonely again."

"I'm going to make sure you stay happy too."

She stopped to kiss him. "I will as long as you stay with me."

He grinned. "Who'd have thought."

"Who'd have thought what?"

"That telling the world the truth about my life would change it."

"You didn't tell the world the truth about your

life. You only told me. And I don't think the truth changed your life as much as it changed you."

"Well, whatever." He glanced around. "So are we keeping this place or what?"

"If Max wants it—"

He laughed. "It might take a couple of million to clean it up and make it work…but we've got a few million hanging around with nothing else to do."

She kissed him again, then led him into the house, up the stairs to the bedroom. If the real estate agent arrived, they never heard him.

But it didn't matter. They weren't selling the ranch. They were keeping it.

And getting chickens.

EPILOGUE

THEY MARRIED THE following year in a spring wedding on the beach. She wore a simple white gown with a veil that was twenty feet long. It brushed the sand, but not often because the light netting caught the breeze and billowed around her more than it fell to the ground. Her old friends from the network had been invited, along with Grant's two best friends. His parents had also come, staying at the beach house with the family. They adored Max. But more than that they wanted a second chance. Grant was now in a place where he knew he had to forgive them. He wasn't there yet. But he was close.

Toward the end of the evening, with guests milling around the pool, drinking wine and dancing to the band tucked in the corner of the pool patio, Caroline came up to them.

"If you don't ditch these people soon, you're not going to get to Paris."

Lola smiled. "I can't wait for Paris."

"With all the times you've taken Max to Janine

and Pierre's, one would think you'd already seen the city."

Grant put his arm around Lola. "We were saving it for our honeymoon."

Caroline rolled her eyes. "Kids. Seriously. What am I going to do with you two?"

"Besides, we might wait a day so we can go to Pierre's first showing in the US."

Caroline rolled her eyes. "He told me over Christmas that no one ever wanted to see his paintings."

Lola laughed. "Times change."

But Grant had also bought a gallery. It didn't hurt to give Max's cousins some motivation to visit more often. Besides, that's what Grant believed money was for. To fill little holes in people's lives.

Lola glanced around. "Times really do change. Look at us. We're very different than we were last year."

Grant caught her hand and twirled her around. "Yes, we are."

Caroline shook her head. "Thanks to Pete Farnsworth."

Grant looked around. "Where is he by the way?"

"In the living room, debating Max about something in his new game. Last time I was in there, he was getting frustrated."

Grant laughed. "Meaning, Max is probably right."

"Apple doesn't fall far from the tree," Lola said.

Caroline laughed. "No, it sure doesn't."

With that she walked away, and Grant laughed. "When are we going to tell her about the new baby?"

Lola leaned in and kissed him. "When we get back…and after we tell Max."

Grant smiled, then slid his arm around her and walked her to the crowd milling around the pool. Never in a million years would he have thought he'd have so many friends, so much love, in his life.

But here he was…the luckiest guy in the world.

* * * * *

*If you enjoyed this story, check out
these other great reads from
Susan Meier*

Claiming His Convenient Princess
Off-Limits to the Rebel Prince
One-Night Baby to Christmas Proposal
His Majesty's Forbidden Fling

All available now!